Labour

ISBN: 9798493802652

First Edition

Content Warnings

This book contains depictions and/or references to mental health issues and symptoms, torture, non-consensual drug use (accidental), psychological and physical abuse, bodily harm, war and murder. It also contains swearing.

Joy is a fight worth winning.

Labours of Stone

Baby vomit pink, Ephra Stone decided. *That's the only way to describe it. It's baby vomit pink.*

Ephra was staring intensely, and with a considerable amount of resentment, at the ceiling of his publisher's polished London office. When he was forced to think about it, Ephra knew it wasn't really the obnoxious shade that Halwyn Tân had chosen to decorate with that made him resent the ceiling's existence. No, it was how often he found himself staring at it, puzzling over the exact right phrase to describe it.

He had never even wanted to be a romance novelist in the first place. Ephra had always intended to write the next great piece of literature. In fact, he had. He'd written a beautiful and immersive 100,000-word tome to rival the *Odyssey*. But no-one would publish it.

His first romance manuscript had been cooked up largely drunk, a week away from eviction, with the sweat of desperation dripping from his brow. When he'd finished, he had taken a walk of shame to his local coffee shop and slipped down the back as quickly as possible. He had settled himself into a corner, laptop out, empty reusable cup on full display, hoping that no-one would notice he hadn't purchased anything before he could log onto the Wi-Fi and send out his query. He had hesitated wildly, telling himself it would be the worst mistake of his career, but inevitably he had pressed send.

Fast forward for what seemed like an eternity, and Ephra was working on his fifth trashy romance novel. The preceding four had contained almost the exact same plot and glove-puppet characters. All he did was re-skin the story with a new setting and different coloured hair. Halwyn loved it. Ephra was his –

"Money-maker!"

Ephra jumped, righting himself in the low bucket seat as Halwyn entered. He tried not to balk at the lilac suit and candyfloss tie the man was wearing, instead grumbling, "Morning, Halwyn."

"Morning!" Halwyn replied brightly, marching around his desk. "Remind me, Ephra, why are you here today?"

Ephra sighed. "You said you had something urgent you wanted to talk to me about."

"Oh!" Halwyn said, then paused, eyeing the contents of his desk. He slammed his hands down, making Ephra jump again. "Oh, yes! I remember now. I wanted to check if you're on track for your draft deadline?"

Ephra grimaced. He wasn't, but that was no reason to drag him across London during Monday morning rush hour. "Halwyn, how is that urgent?"

"Because, Ephra, I thought I'd pre-empt the little tantrum we had last time, make sure there are no 'messes' heading my way, and remind you you're under contract and –"

"And if I don't get a wiggle on, you'll cancel our contract and ask for my advance back." He mimicked Halwyn's broad Welsh accent. "Yes, Halwyn, I know. And you promised me you wouldn't bring up last time."

Halwyn lowered his voice. "I might well have done, but there's no need to be a prick about it, Ephra. You make me a lot of money, but you know I won't tolerate bullying. What's the company motto?"

Ephra rolled his eyes. "We *love* love."

"Yes, we love love. Not mocking imitations of our colleagues."

Ephra took a deep breath in and slowly released it through his teeth. "I'm sorry, Halwyn."

"Thank you." Halwyn grinned at him. Sometimes, out of the corner of his eye, Ephra could swear the whole row of teeth looked like fangs. "Now, how is the book going?"

"It's going."

"So you've not written anything yet?"

Ephra knocked the heel of his shoe against the magenta carpet. "Not yet, no."

"Right, well then. I'll have a thousand words by tomorrow morning, please."

"You've got to be joking!"

"I couldn't be further from joking, Ephra. This time the cancellation threat is very real. Management are beginning to question if the amount you bring in balances against the overtime they pay me to chase you. So I am going to get you on track. Do you understand?"

Ephra growled and began to scramble out of the low chair with little grace. He shook out his long coat and smoothed down the lapels, then remembered how short the coat made him look and wished he'd stayed seated.

"Ephra, I asked you a question."

"God, Hal! Yes! *Fine*, you'll have your bloody book on time!" Ephra snarled. "But do me a favour and get rid of the baby vomit on the ceiling, will you? It's driving me batty."

Halwyn looked up in confusion. "What baby vomit?"

Ephra growled again and stalked out of the office.

As he always did after a crummy meeting with Halwyn, Ephra got off the tube at Knightsbridge Station, bought a terrible and incredibly expensive coffee from the high street, and made a rapid beeline north towards the park.

He headed straight for the edge of the Serpentine, slowing down with a deep exhalation the moment he saw the water.

It was November and the air was bitter, but the sky was crystal clear. There weren't many people wandering around the park in the middle of Monday morning, but a couple of boats full of rowers cut through the glassy water, sending waves skittering across the surface. Ephra stopped for a moment and watched them speed along. He imagined what it would be like to feel the cold air whistling across his broad cheek bones, tousling through his dark, scraped-back hair. He yearned to be out there with the rowers, but of course, he didn't even know how to swim.

He took a swig of his coffee, made a face, and began to stroll along the underbelly of the Serpentine, his ultimate goal a scraggy old flat above a shop in Bayswater. He made a lot of money for Halwyn, yes, but the contract he'd signed had been for five small advance payments and crappy royalties. It was more money than most writers made, but most writers weren't pumped like machines.

Ephra shook his head clear. He had to stop thinking about work when he wasn't working. He had to try and find some joy in life again. He took another sip of coffee. *Finding a better coffee shop should also be on the priority list*, he thought. His stomach growled. *I guess food would be good as well.*

He plodded along a bit further before musing aloud, "Maybe a little love for myself would be quite nice, too."

A fluffy little song thrush perched on the fence chutted at him. Ephra stopped. He quickly looked around to check no-one was coming and then said, "No, not really. I don't think I've ever been in love."

The bird chirped at him again. Ephra frowned. "Well, to have been in love you have to have found someone, connected with them, said the words, and then you have to be willing to fight for that, right? But I'm knocking on thirty and terminally single. Every time I meet someone and think, *maybe, maybe this will work,* something gets in the way."

"Tweet?" The thrush turned its head, as if asking a question.

"Sometimes it's a new job on the other side of the planet, other times the one that got away comes back right as things are getting interesting. The last time an actual *war* started up the day I was going to tell this soldier guy I was seeing that I wanted to be exclusive. I was a wreck after that one." Ephra took a deep breath. Moaning at some poor bird wasn't really helping anything. "Sorry, little fella. I'm being miserable, aren't I?" Ephra looked around again, and offered the song thrush his finger.

He found the birds in Hyde Park and Kensington Gardens were alarmingly tame. They often landed on him if he stood still long enough, and despite how frequently he vented his frustration to them, they rarely flew away. The thrush hopped up onto his finger. Ephra put his coffee down next to the railing and petted his new feathered friend with his thumb.

Halwyn's motto, 'We love love,' span around Ephra's head. The truth was that Ephra Stone, the great romance novelist, didn't 'love love'. Ephra didn't even *know* love.

Ephra scoffed, shook himself again, and said to the bird, "I *really* need to stop thinking about work. No wonder I can never get any sleep."

The thrush chirped twice and then fluttered off his hand. Ephra grabbed his coffee. When he looked up again, the bird was back on the fence. It chirped and hopped away a little. He took a step forward and it flew off. Ephra felt a strange impulse to see where it was going. He jogged steadily after it, until it disappeared into the landscaping next to the *Serenity* statue.

Ephra came to a halt, panting. *Well, that was silly*, he thought. *At least I got some exercise in, though.*

He took a moment to admire the shining green statue in the morning light, then took the path to the right, along the river's edge, craving the extra breeze off the water. He was almost to the Serpentine Bridge when he heard the first yell.

"Sticks! Sticks! Where are you, Sticks?!" It was a male voice coming from the block of bushes and trees to his left, where the song thrush had hidden itself.

Surely there's no shortage of sticks in there? Ephra mused and snorted.

Then a man came tumbling out before him; a tall, lean, sun-kissed god, with a flop of unkempt curls. Ephra had about a second to think, *Oh, no*, before reaching out an arm to stop the poor guy from falling straight into the river. He launched his terrible coffee into the water in the process.

"Shhhhugar," said the man. "Oh, good heavens. I'm sorry! Are you alright? Oh, no, your coffee. I'm so sorry!"

Ephra blinked at him, unable to think anything other than, *Oh, no. No, no, no. I didn't really mean it. Stupid bird. No.*

The man smiled at him all the same. He straightened himself up a bit, pulling his T-shirt back down where it had rucked up over his hip. Then he offered Ephra a hand.

"Thank you for saving me from my swan dive, there. I'm Ron." *No, no, no.* "And you are?"

"*Ephra*," Ephra squeaked, then cleared his throat and said again in a much deeper voice, "Ephra. Sorry."

"Nice to meet you." Ron waggled his hand at him. Ephra took it. The shake was firm and friendly.

Oh, fuck. Just don't be a soldier.

"Say, uh, you don't happen to have seen, um… " Ron trailed off. "Oh, no. Never mind."

"H-have you lost your dog?" Ephra asked, fearing the man with *that face* might turn away.

"I –" Ron grinned. "Yes, I have lost my dog. Her name is Sticks."

"Well, uh, I don't have very much on for the rest of the day." Halwyn and his thousand words could rot for all Ephra cared. "I could help you look for her?"

Ron chuckled. "Bit out of character for a Londoner. You're not a weirdo, are you?" He winked.

Ephra did his best not to swoon. "Oh, no. I'm, uh, I'm posh Brummie. People get more helpful the further North you go." Ephra gave himself a mental pat on the back for remembering how to converse with strangers.

Ron laughed, and his dark gold curls bounced with mirth. Ephra swallowed hard.

"Actually, I'd be grateful for the help. Sticks can be an absolute pain in the backside to find. Blends right in," Ron explained.

Ephra nodded. "What does she look like?"

"Oh, hmm," Ron thought for a moment. "She's sort of grey and speckled. Quite big, but not in a plump way … more in a long way."

"Long?" Ephra raised a brow.

"Yes, long. Very long."

"What about her coat? Short hair, long hair?" Ephra asked.

"No hair."

"No hair?"

"Yup."

"So you're looking for a very long, grey, hairless dog?"

"Indeed." Ron nodded a little too eagerly.

Ah, Ephra thought, staring at the beautiful bloke before him in wonder. "You've lost a snake, haven't you?"

Ron chewed over his bottom lip, and then threw up his hands. "Yes! Yes! Okay, I lost my snake. She slipped out when I went to get milk, and she always heads down this way."

"She *always* heads down this way?" Ephra boggled at the idea that this man regularly lost a snake in the middle of London. Surely *someone* would have mentioned to him that a huge great snake liked to stroll along the Serpentine from time to time.

"I mean, not here exactly. Sticks likes Long Water, too. But she does have a thing for the Serpentine."

"And you thought I was the weirdo?" Ephra jibed.

Ron's smile dropped. "Look, it's okay if you don't want to help or whatever. I get it. Snakes aren't for everyone." He began to plod back into the bushes.

Ephra felt a bolt of something shoot threw him.

16

You absolute pillock.

"No, no!" He leapt after Ron. "I'll help! I quite like snakes." Ephra actually had no fixed opinion on snakes (that he knew of), but his gut told him that Ron was worth getting to know. "We'll find her together, don't worry."

They spent the morning scouring the carefully crafted landscape of Hyde Park. By noon, there was still no sign of the elusive Sticks, and Ephra was ravenous, so he bought them both a sandwich at one of the park's many cafes and they sat with their backs to the water, watching the trees while they ate.

Ephra did his best not to make a mess of himself, pulling his sandwich apart section by section, feeding it to himself in bite-sized chunks. It felt a bit odd, but the last thing he wanted was to get mayonnaise down his wool coat in front of a perfect, *very perfect*, stranger. Ron, however, munched his food with reckless abandon. Every time he took a bite he smiled to himself. Ephra couldn't help but smile with him.

"Enjoying that?" Ephra pointed.

"Yes, thank you ever so much!" Ron answered around a mouthful of bread and ham. He paused, chewed and swallowed. "I didn't even realise I was hungry. I so often forget to eat these days."

"Stress?" Ephra asked.

"Oh, no. I wouldn't say that." His cheeks reddened a little. "Honestly, I'm just a bit terrible at remembering how to human." He laughed nervously. "I take excellent care of Sticks, though! I keep her fed and she has plenty of space for a snake of her size."

Ephra raised his hands. "Hey, hey! No judgement here. I'm sure you're a great snake parent or whatever the term is."

Ron visibly relaxed. "I like to think of myself as her guardian. You can't really tell a snake what to do, you know? She's not a child. You have to let her do her own thing and try to keep trouble away."

Ephra popped the last section of his sandwich into his mouth and scrunched the paper bag up in his hands. "So, you treat her like ... a friend?"

Ron wiped his whole arm across his face to remove a smidge of butter from his chin. It didn't work. Ephra tried not to laugh and passed him a napkin from his pocket. Once clean, Ron answered, "I know it's weird, but Sticks is ... well, she's smart and wilful. You'll see when we find her."

He tossed the napkin into his empty sandwich bag and folded it all up together.

"Did you want to try up by Long Water? She

doesn't seem to be around here," Ephra suggested. He took Ron's litter and dropped it in the bin. When he turned back, Ron looked fretful. "What's wrong?"

"It's … this is the longest she's been missing, you know? Normally, I come out here and I find her right where we met." Ron's eyes started searching the trees nearest to them as he spoke. "Or, I suppose sometimes she's up by the Peter Pan statue. She does like scaring the kids."

Ephra blinked in surprise. "And she's never been reported to the RSPCA?"

"No, of course not! She only scares the kids, she never lets the parents see her."

"Very smart."

"Oh, very, very smart. She's probably smarter than I am."

Ephra chuckled at that, and patted Ron gently on the back. "Come on then, let's head up that way."

Ron let out a sigh, accidentally slumping into Ephra's side. "Sorry," he said, but he didn't really move away. "I just hope we find her before it gets dark."

By the time the sun started to set over London, Ephra and Ron had made it to the Italian Gardens at the northern end of Long Water. Sticks had not been lurking near Peter Pan, nor had they managed to spot her amongst any of the shrubs, trees, and bushes. Poor Ron was getting more and more anxious. Ephra could see it in the way he was holding himself, like his rib cage had collapsed under the weight of his shoulders. He wanted to comfort him, but Ephra had never really comforted anyone. Not that he could remember. And even if he had the ability, wouldn't it be weird coming from him, some random stranger?

There, there, Ephra played with the words, *I'm sure she's alright. Maybe she went home? You said she was smart.*

He bit his tongue at the idea of a homing snake. Even he knew laughing right now was a dickish thing to do.

Ron came to a halt in front of the pump house and yelled at the top of his voice. "*Sticks! This isn't funny anymore. We need to go home! Sticks!*"

When no snake appeared, Ron slumped against one of the pump house columns and slid down to the floor. His fingers knotted into his hair. Ephra squatted down next to him. "Hey," he found himself saying. "Hey, it'll be alright."

"No it won't!" Ron said. "I have to find her, Ephra. I can't leave her out here. It's too cold, and she might fall into the water."

"Can't snakes swim?" Ephra asked, dumbly.

"Yes! That's the problem. If she gets into the water she could end up anywhere!" Ron let out a noise, somewhere between a sob and a grunt of frustration. "She could *already* be anywhere!"

"I'm sorry, Ron."

"I'm going to be in so much trouble." Ron shook his head mercilessly. "I can't have lost her. I just can't."

"Trouble?"

Ron blinked, looking up at Ephra like he was the one who'd said something bizarre.

"You said you'll be in trouble if you can't find her?" Ephra repeated.

Ron looked at his shoes and began picking at the canvas. "She's, uh, she's a big part of my job. If I lose Sticks, then I'll have to cancel all of my appointments until I find her."

Ephra resisted the urge to ask what job Ron did that required a snake. He also bit back the suggestion that Ron simply get another snake. Ephra sensed it wasn't the time for either of those conversations. Instead, he said, "Okay. Right. Well, we haven't searched this bit properly yet, so why don't you sit here and I'll have a look around."

"I'll come," Ron said, and began lifting himself up.

Ephra planted a hand on Ron's shoulder and pushed him back down. "Sit," he commanded in his most

21

assertive tone. "You need to take a break. Okay?"

Ron sniffed. "Okay."

Ephra gave Ron's shoulder a quick squeeze. It was meant to be comforting, but Ephra couldn't help but notice how muscular Ron felt beneath his fingers. He shook himself, and started working his way around the garden's four ponds.

The place was pretty much dead already. There were a few people speeding their way along the footpaths, but no-one was interested in the Italian Gardens when the sun was on its way out. There wasn't really a light source in the park beyond London's normal amber glow and the last remnants of daylight. Ephra got his phone out and turned on the torch function. As he searched, he noticed how eerily calm and black the pools were, how silent everything felt. He felt pretty warm in his long wool coat, but he couldn't help but shiver. Suddenly, it felt like the world had ended, and he was the only one left.

The moment the thought occurred, he span around and looked back towards the pump house. Ron waved in the torchlight. Ephra breathed a sigh of relief.

What are you scared of? Puddles?

He snaked his way around the pools on the right, then turned towards the sculpted fountain. He studied every inch of the floor, the water, the carved stone. It was only as he was about to move onto the left side of the garden that he heard a gentle *hissssss.*

Ephra span on his heel and was greeted by a pair of silvery eyes and a flickering tongue. The great scaled head lifted up from the wall as the snake studied Ephra meticulously. Ron hadn't been joking when he said she was big. Her grey speckled body appeared endless, disappearing into the darkness at the edge of Ephra's torchlight. She was, simply put, enormous.

Ephra's lungs began to burn, and he realised that he hadn't taken a breath in a long time. He also realised that he'd forgotten how to breathe. The snake leant towards him and for a moment he could have sworn he saw a look of recognition in her beady eyes. Then, she slid herself around his shoulders and draped her great body gracefully over his arms.

"*Ron*," Ephra squeaked. "*RON!*"

On the second yell, there was a mad scuffle of feet. Ephra turned the phone gently around in his hand to light himself.

"Sticks!" Ron yelled excitedly.

Ephra stiffened. He was standing in a rigid T-pose, unable to move. "Please, don't yell at the giant snake while she is still attached to my body."

Ron laughed a little, clearly in a much better mood. "Oh, she won't bite, will you, Sitcks?"

The snake hissed again, and Ephra felt the flicker of her tongue against his ear. "Please, Ron. Please get her off me."

Ephra knew that the look on his face was one of
sheer panic. Normally, he would have been thoroughly
embarrassed, but right at that precise moment, he was
more concerned about being eaten by an endless
monstrosity.

Ron laughed again, but gently wrapped his hand
around Ephra's wrist. "Come on, wriggle monster. I
know he's nice and hot, but it's time we went home."

Ephra felt the snake's muscles bend and flex as she
laced her way off his shoulders and onto Ron's arm.
When the end of her tail slipped from his fingers, it was
everything he could do not to immediately drop to the
floor. He stumbled back against the garden wall, gripped
his thighs with his hands and let out a long shuddering
breath.

Ephra sensed Ron sauntering up to him, but
couldn't look up. He'd think about being polite when his
skin stopped crawling.

"*Fudge.* I'm sorry, Ephra. Why didn't you say you
were this scared of snakes?" Ron asked.

Ephra panted for a few seconds longer, then said, "I
didn't know ... she was ... so big."

"Big?" Ron said baffled. "I mean, she's pretty long,
but she's only four foot and skinny as anything."

"What?!" Ephra snapped. "She's huge! She's –" He
stopped dead in the middle of his sentence. As he flicked

his phone torch up at Ron, what he saw around Ron's arm was not the mammoth speckled serpent he'd seen before. She was relatively large, yes, but comfortably sized for handling. "That's – that's impossible," Ephra stuttered. "She was so much bigger."

Ron shrugged as Sticks wound her way around the back of his neck and nestled her head atop his curls. "Maybe it was the light?" he suggested.

Ephra couldn't take his eyes off the snake. His breathing was calmer, but still forceful.

Ron reached out to him. "Come on, you've had a scare and it's my fault. Come back to mine and I'll make you a cuppa."

Ephra flinched, worried that Sticks might suddenly grow again, or slither back onto him, but then he let himself look at Ron's face. He was squinting with the light in his eyes, but Ephra could see his tentative smile and genuine remorse. Ephra's heart did a little leap. He couldn't remember the last time anyone had looked that concerned for him, so he held out his arm and let Ron tow him home.

The trek back to Ron's took about twenty-five minutes. It was quite dark and strangely intimate. Ron didn't let go of Ephra's arm once, steering him along the edge of the water with the ease and grace of something nocturnal. At one point, Ephra had offered Ron his phone's torch, but Ron had simply said, "It's okay. Save your battery. I know the way."

Sticks had hissed in agreement. Ephra had rapidly tucked his phone away inside his coat.

At the park exit, they paused for a minute to adjust to the brightness, then Ron pointed across the main road into Knightsbridge. "I'm just down there."

When Ron finally stopped outside a four storey London townhouse and let go of Ephra's arm to get his keys out of his pocket, Ephra let out a chuckle of disbelief.

"This can't be your place!" he said.

Ron grinned. "I know, it's a bit small, but it was all I could afford when I moved here."

"*Small?!*" Ephra repeated. "How much did it cost you? Five million?"

Ron shrank, clearly realising he'd misinterpreted Ephra's comment. "Eight," he corrected, and headed up the stone steps to unlock the front door. Sticks dropped down his back a little, apparently watching Ephra's reaction.

Ephra stared up at the building and whistled. "Eight million pounds. *Eight million pounds.*" He wondered if he'd see eight million pass through his hands in his whole lifetime.

Ron cleared his throat from the doorway. "Are you coming in?"

"Yes! Sorry." Ephra shook off his wonder and raced up the stairs.

He occasionally spent a few hours flicking through London house listings online, mainly for writing research, to add a bit of setting colour. Most of the houses had wide open rooms, styled very modern or very regal. There was never any in-between, and they always seemed sterile, either way. Ron's house, however, was warm and cosy, a myriad of terracotta and chocolate tones mixed with dark and red woodwork. Ephra felt immediately at home.

"Can I take your coat?" Ron asked.

"Oh, uh, I can put it somewhere if you point me in the right direction. I imagine you want to put Sticks away." Ephra gestured to Sticks' head, now perched on Ron's shoulder, her body still coiled around his arm.

Ron gently stroked her scaly spine. "I suppose I should. You could use some time under your heat lamp, couldn't you?" She pushed her nose against his cheek as if she were a cat. "You can put your coat in the hall cupboard if you like. There's some hangers in there." He pointed to the door.

"Will do."

"When you're done, come through to the living

room. I'll bring you that cuppa I promised."

Ephra nodded and watched Ron walk away. He caught himself before his gaze could travel inappropriately south and turned to the cupboard. Ephra opened it, found a hanger and hung up his coat, fastening a button so that it wouldn't fall off. There were a large number of shoes strewn about the bottom, and he didn't want to risk the wool getting muddy.

When he entered the living room, Ron was placing Sticks into a tank that spanned the entire width of the room and rose to the height of the tall man's hip. It was filled with bark and logs and a giant ceramic water dish. Everything looked pristine, beautifully clean. In contrast, the rest of the space was a bit of a shambles, but not unbearably so.

"Wow, that's a big tank." Ephra tottered over two stacks of books and an empty glass to Ron's side.

"Yes, they say to keep snakes her size in something smaller, but she likes the extra stretching space." As if to prove Ron's point, Sticks lay herself out in a long straight line across the bottom of the tank. Ephra peered at Ron. There was so much affection on his face, it was mesmerising. Ron caught him looking and his golden skin blushed. "Sorry," he said. "You don't know what it means to see her safely back at home."

Ephra nudged him with his elbow, gripped the edge of the tank and looked back down at Sticks. "I can imagine, though. And, well, it's nice to see a smile on your face."

Ron placed his hand over Ephra's and squeezed it slightly. "Seriously, thank you. I don't know what I would have done today without your help."

Ephra shrugged, not daring to let himself look at Ron. His stomach was doing somersaults at Ron's touch. "Well, I couldn't not help. And it's not like I had anything more important to do."

Ron squeezed his hand again, then moved away. "Right, tea!" he said brightly. "I'll be back in a minute."

Ephra looked up and grinned at the back of Ron's blond head. He smiled so hard his cheeks felt sore. When Ron was out of sight, he looked down at Sticks and she looked up at him.

"I don't know what I saw in the dark," he said to her. "But I guess I should thank you for getting lost today. I really like Ron."

Ephra could have sworn the snake smiled. Then she slithered over to her water dish. As she dipped her nose into the water, the reflection seemed to change. For a very brief moment, it looked like a face, but then Sticks' scaly body broke it up as she coiled herself around. Ephra blinked rapidly. *Lord, I'm tired,* he thought.

"Here you go!" Ron chirped, returning with two great mugs and an assortment of milk, sugar and sweeteners. "I wasn't sure how you took it, so I brought everything with me."

"That's great." Ephra followed him across the room as they climbed and traversed the small piles of stuff dotted about the place.

"I'm sorry about the mess," Ron said as he sat down and shunted some magazines off the table to make room for the tea tray. "I normally tidy things up in the morning ready for clients in the afternoon, but then Sticks –"

"It's okay, you don't have to apologise," Ephra cut him off. "And besides, I've seen far worse in my own flat."

Ron looked surprised. "That seems unlikely."

"Oh, I'm clean shaven and well-oiled now, but I was a complete mess for a good long while." Ephra poured a spot of milk into the mug nearest to him, added some sugar and began to stir. "I still am really, but my publisher is all about appearances. Can't have his best writer looking like a hermit."

"You're a writer?!" Ron asked. "Anything I would know?"

Ephra let his head sink between his shoulders. He hadn't meant to let that one slip so soon. "Probably not." He took the spoon out of his tea. "I'm one of those hacky romance novelists. Doomed to write the same story over and over and over."

"Oh, but come on now. Those are some of the best books!"

Ephra raised a brow. "You've got to be joking."

"No! I think they're wonderful. Everyone needs a lovey-dovey cheese-fest from time to time."

Ephra sat back on the sofa and looked Ron in the eye. "Wow, you're actually serious."

Ron grinned and pointed to the book case on the far wall. "That entire thing is trash: romance, sci-fi, crime, etc., etc. None of the 'good' stuff. Only the stuff that's been done a million times before. Each and every one of them is absolute gold."

Ephra smiled a little at Ron's enthusiasm. "Okay." He paused. "I guess it's pretty nice to hear that, actually."

"I bet I have one of your books! What's your penname?"

Ephra winced. "It's just E Stone, but you don't –"

Ron jumped up and leapt across the room, retrieving four little pink paperbacks, all of which appeared to have been read multiple times. "See!" Ron laughed, plonking himself back down next to Ephra. "Your books are great! They've got such wonderful rhythm. It's really soothing."

"Soothing?"

"Yes! They're predictable, easy, satisfying, like pushing an oar through the water. You know where you're going. That's comforting." He grabbed Ephra's shoulder and jostled him lightly, his eyes shining with glee. "You'll have to sign all of these for me, you know that, right?"

Ephra rolled his eyes, but not with his usual sarcasm. He was giddy with second-hand excitement. "If I have to," he said, joy all over his face.

Ron clapped and shoved his hand down the side of the sofa. After a moment's shuffling, he retrieved a slightly lint-covered pen, which he wiped across his jeans and handed to Ephra, bouncing ever so slightly too close. Ephra took the pen, trying not to think about the warmth he could feel radiating from Ron's skin. He flicked open the first book, *No Love Unturned.*

"Do you want me to write anything special?" Ephra asked.

"Surprise me."

Ephra took a couple of seconds to think, then wrote:

Thanks for saving me from your giant-arse snake.

Love,
Ephra Stone.

Ron snorted, reading over his shoulder.

Ephra put the book to one side and flicked open the cover of *As Hard as Love.* Knowing that Ron was watching sent a little thrill through his body. He licked his lips at the flurry of thoughts that swept through his mind. There were a lot of things he wanted to write, but he'd known Ron for less than a day. He couldn't let himself get carried away by golden curls and that ridiculous smile.

I'm glad to have met you, my number one fan.

Love,
Ephra Stone.

Ron leant in further, trying to get a better view of Ephra's handwriting. *As Hard as Love*'s title page was crowded by a black and white photo of a random couple getting passionate, so Ephra had written the inscription smaller. Ron took the book from his hands, grazing Ephra's palm with his fingers.

"I shall hold that title with pride," he said. Ephra chanced a quick look. Ron was very, very close, grinning into the pages of the book.

Ephra took a long breath, as steadily as he could. Then he picked up *A Rolling Love*. Knowing that Ron was still thumbing *As Hard as Love*, he felt a spark of bravery and wrote:

I don't usually like most people, but you've made me laugh more in one day than I have in a year.

Love,
Ephra Stone.

He put the book down with the cover closed and quickly picked up *Set in Love*, the last book. Before he could let himself overthink it, he scrawled out his final inscription, shut the book and tucked it under *A Rolling Love*.

"All done," he said, and placed the pen next to the stack of pink books. He picked up his mug of tea and watched out of the corner of his eye as Ron put down *As Hard as Love* and took the next novel from the table.

"Ephra …" Ron said warmly as he read the note. He placed a hand on Ephra's knee and their arms pressed together gently. "I'm glad I could bring you a little laughter, even if I did scare the sugar out of you with Sticks."

Ephra didn't reply. He took a sip of tea and tapped the cover of the next book. Ron picked it up. There was complete silence as Ron read and re-read the final message. Ephra was trying to estimate how quickly he could collect his coat and bolt when Ron reached out and took the mug from his hands. He placed it neatly on the tea tray before tilting Ephra's face towards him.

"You sure you want to know?" Ron asked, a cheeky grin on his face.

There was a long pause in which they both sat frozen, faces inches away from each other, sharing one shaky breath after another.

"Uh-huh," was all Ephra could manage.

Ron tentatively brushed his lips against Ephra's and Ephra's heart exploded in his chest, his whole body lighting up like a brand-new solar system. When Ron did it again, Ephra followed him as he retreated, scuffing their noses together. Ron chuckled and Ephra felt it, realising his hand had already knotted itself into the bottom of Ron's T-shirt. Ephra shivered, closed his eyes, and that's when Ron kissed him properly.

Ephra gasped at the pleasant pressure, and Ron's tongue flicked the tip of his own. He felt strong arms wrap around his torso and dip him back into the sofa cushions. Ephra didn't think he had ever felt this out of control, like he was spinning down a mountain, unable to get his grip. He slid his hand up into Ron's curls and tugged. Ron let a small moan slip into Ephra's mouth. He nipped Ephra's bottom lip, before pulling away slightly.

"Have I sated your curiosity yet?" Ron said, a little breathless.

Ephra swallowed and shook his head. "No, absolutely not."

"More research required?"

"Yes." Ephra guided Ron gently back towards him.

Set in Love sat open to the inscription on the coffee table. The hasty scrawl read:

I would very much like to know what that smile of yours tastes like.

Love,
Ephra Stone.

The pair kissed each other into a dreamlike bubble of endorphins, then talked themselves awake again. Ron was impossibly easy to talk to, and Ephra soon found himself recounting how he came to write *No Love Unturned* at his lowest point, and how he'd felt trapped in a world of pastels that he wasn't really built for ever since.

"I can sympathise with that," Ron said. "I always wanted to be a sailor, to go off on some epic adventure, but my family had 'more realistic' ideas for my future."

Ephra made an 'ugh' noise and smoothed his thumb along Ron's jaw.

"Sticks makes it worth it, though," Ron whispered. "I'd do anything for her. You just have to find the thing that makes it worth it."

Ephra studied the grey-blue flecks in Ron's eyes and couldn't help but think how profoundly strong Ron's kindness was; how merciless his joy; how awesome his laughter.

I'm starting to sound like an actual romantic, Ephra scoffed at himself.

"What?" Ron shoved him.

"It's not you, it's not you! I promise," he said. "Well, maybe it is you. I was painting pretty word pictures in my head and normally it's a mangle of clichés, but I think you might have added something new to the mix."

Ron smiled, and kissed Ephra very gently. Ephra practically purred. And then he remembered the thousand words he needed to send Halwyn the next day.

Ron noticed the change in his expression immediately. He stroked one long index finger along Ephra's frown line and said, "What's this thought, here?"

"I've just remembered I have work due tomorrow." Ephra sighed.

Ron growled pathetically. "Oh, Pixy Stix."

"Don't you ever swear like a normal person?"

Ron flushed red. "I deal with a lot of people from a lot of places, so I try not to use profanities. Some of them *really* don't like it."

"Okay, fair." Ephra smiled. "Are you going to let

me up?"

Ron leant up, surveying their position. They were lying on the sofa facing each other, but Ron had his long legs tangled between Ephra's, one foot propped on the coffee table, the other drooping to the floor.

He grinned. "Would you hate me if I said no?"

Ephra chuckled. "No, but my publisher would have a problem with it. And then you might not ever get to read my next inscription." He added a wink for good measure and his own flirtation made his insides knot up.

Fuck me, that's a feeling, Ephra thought.

Ron let out another growl as he lifted one leg from the top of the pile. This freed Ephra's right leg, but Ron still had his left pinned to the seat. Ephra looked at him quizzically.

"Got to pay the toll if you want your full freedom," Ron explained.

"Toll?"

Ron tapped his lips, his face glowing with mischief. Ephra feigned annoyance and kissed him deeply. "Say when," he mumbled into his mouth.

"Never," Ron murmured back.

Both of them laughed, and Ephra toppled over backwards onto a pile of books, his trapped foot wedging itself under Ron's knee. There was a pause before they both spluttered with laughter again.

It took a second or two for the pair to stop giggling

like school boys – every time they glanced at each other, it set them off again – but when they finally recovered, Ron helped Ephra up and walked him to the door. He retrieved Ephra's coat from the hall cupboard, offering it to him hesitantly. Ephra took it from him with a similar reluctance. Once he was snugly wrapped back up in wool, they stared at each other wistfully, neither really wanting the night to end.

"I, uh, I guess I should get going. It's a long walk back now the park's closed." Ephra scuffed the toe of his shoe against the hard wood floor.

"Number!" Ron jumped and did a mad dash over to his small hall table. He pulled open a drawer. "Hang on. Yup, there they are." He returned with a business card that read:

Ron Brook
Alternative Mediation Services

And then listed his phone number and e-mail address. Ephra made a show of tucking the card into the hidden pocket in his coat, the one with a little button to stop things from falling out.

"I will definitely call you," Ephra said. "I can't believe I have to leave because of a sodding book."

Ron smoothed a loose strand of Ephra's hair back into place. "It's okay. I'm sure there will be other nights."

They kissed once more, and again for good luck, and then Ephra dragged himself down Ron's front steps and out of Knightsbridge, before his resolve could dissolve. When he hit the edge of the park, he headed west and then north, up into Bayswater. He couldn't decide if he was moving so fast because he was cold, or because he actually felt happy for once. *How is it that one stranger can make the world feel bright again?*

Forty minutes alone with his own thoughts, and the only negative he could find in the whole evening was being confronted by a giant snake, which turned out to be a reasonably sized snake, apparently. Ephra couldn't rid himself of the image of that great head staring at him in the darkness, but he knew he'd seen perfectly normal-sized Sticks in good light. Snakes couldn't just shrink like that. It had to have been a trick of the light.

That issue solved, he kicked open the door to his flat and immediately headed into the kitchen, where he dumped his coat and picked up his laptop. Ignoring the angry growl of his stomach, he made his way into the living room and promptly flopped into his armchair. He checked the cup on his side table; it still contained that morning's black coffee, which was of course stone cold, but Ephra didn't really care. He had writing to do, and he'd take the caffeine where he could get it.

He coughed and spluttered. His mouth tasted of dirt and blood. He was lying face down on the ground. As he tried to lift himself up, the wet mud beneath him gave way and he slipped. Pain rocketed through his body as his stomach connected with the earth. He reached down, tenderly prodding his way across his abdomen. What he felt made him scream.

He took a shuddering breath and rolled himself over. There was no way he'd make it back to the trenches. Even if he did, he'd only add to the clutter of the dead and the dying, getting in the way of those still fighting. Better to die out in the open, under the stars. Better to witness something beautiful as he slid into darkness.

He saw the shadow of something floating across the sky. It was a bird with an enormous wingspan. Maybe a heron. He watched it flit gracefully amongst the tiny dots of light, barely visible. Then he heard the whistle of a bomb.

"Watch out!" he yelled to the bird, then everything went black.

Ephra woke with a start to the synthetic melody of his mobile phone. His laptop fell off his lap and clattered onto the floor as he dug through his trouser pockets for the blasted device.

"Shit," he said, but made no actual effort to check if the laptop was okay.

He dragged his phone out of his pocket, noted the time was 9AM and looked at the caller ID. Halwyn Tân.

Of course it's him, Ephra grunted, then answered.

"What?" he said with a voice that sounded like it had slept on hot coals.

"Morning, Money-maker!" Halwyn responded. Ephra held the phone away from his ear; Halwyn was always too loud, at any time of day. "How are you feeling? Did you get a good night's sleep?"

"You know I didn't." Ephra growled. He had sent Halwyn his thousand words at four o'clock in the morning, completely unedited, squeezed fresh from the stone.

"Oh!" Halwyn said, innocently. "I thought that said 4PM, not 4AM. Heavens above, did I wake you?"

Ephra sighed. "Yes, Hal. You did."

"I'm terribly sorry, Ephra." Halwyn tutted at

himself. Ephra doubted that Halwyn was ever truly sorry about anything, let alone waking him up. "It's just I read your pages and I *had* to talk to you about them as soon as possible."

Ephra leant forward in his seat and rubbed his face with his palm, trying to shake off the last vapours of his nightmare. If he was honest, he couldn't really remember what he'd written the night before. All he could remember was … was Ron. Ephra smiled. "Yes, go on?"

"Oh, well, I wanted to congratulate you on how enthusiastic they were! They felt … they felt truly inspired, Ephra. Almost as if you enjoyed writing them?"

Ephra picked his laptop up off the floor and tapped the button to wake it. Last night's words came up on the screen. As he skimmed he realised he'd written a petite dark-haired young heroine falling for a lean, bronzed hero with billowing golden curls. His morning gloom slid right off and Ephra laughed at himself.

"Ephra?"

"Sorry, Hal, I'm refreshing my memory. Still a bit blurry-eyed."

"Of course, of course! But yes, I wanted to ask, is this something you're enjoying?" There was something about Halwyn's tone that sounded … wrong. Ephra couldn't figure out what it was, but it sounded rather like someone was playing Halwyn's voice in a minor key.

"Yes, I guess I did enjoy writing it. Anything

wrong with that?" Ephra asked.

Halwyn cleared his throat, and the next words rang out in his usual happy lilt. "Oh, absolutely not! I just wondered what's changed?"

There was no way on this Earth that Ephra was going to tell Halwyn about Ron. *Ron.* Thinking the name at that precise moment made Ephra's facial features spasm in confusion. He wanted to grin so badly, but Halwyn's prying was infuriating.

"Look, Hal," Ephra began, landing firmly on annoyance. "I appreciate the positive feedback, I do. It's always nice to hear, but I don't see how what goes on in my life is any of your business."

That seemed to leave Halwyn a bit breathless. The only reason Ephra didn't ask if he was still there was because he could hear the background noise of the office. Eventually Halwyn said, "Apologies, Ephra, an urgent e-mail caught my eye. But you're quite right, I shouldn't pry! It's not as if you're heartbroken and refusing to write again." He paused. The hair on the back of Ephra's neck prickled. "I would like to request the rest of this chapter and the next by the weekend, though."

Ephra grimaced. "Yeah, sure. I can get that to you."

"You can?" Halwyn sounded surprised. "Because that would be great. We'd be right on track for full submission."

"Yes, Hal." Ephra cleared his throat, thought of

Ron, and said brightly, "I can absolutely do that."

Ephra knew the man was gobsmacked because, for the first time in all the time Ephra had known him, Halwyn's voice got awfully quiet. "Right, well then. I look forward to hearing from you."

"And I look forward to your feedback. Bye, Hal."

"Yes. Goodbye, Ephra."

Ephra hung up and sat back in his chair. He was still a little frustrated, but the image of Halwyn Tân, sat in his vomit-inducing office, trying to string a thought together after that conversation, made him chuckle. Even when Ephra was doggedly single, he was a nightmare to coax through a novel. More than once, Halwyn had had to come and sit in the flat to make sure he was actually working.

This time, though, Ephra thought, picking up his laptop, *I think I really am going to* love *love.*

Ephra knocked out the rest of the chapter in about an hour, then gathered his bones and forced himself out of the armchair. The noise he made was rather alarming. *But that is what happens when you sleep in daft places*, he told himself. He stretched in something resembling tree pose before wobbling into the kitchen to make himself a bowl of cereal.

He didn't get that far, though. The sight of his coat on the table had him scrambling through his pockets for Ron's card. Once found, he read the beautiful black embossed letters again and again, ran his thumb over the indents and pressed the card to his lips.

Then he thought about how much of a tit he must look, and proceeded to grin like an absolute tool.

He skidded back into the living room and grabbed his phone off the table. He could text, he should text. *That's the etiquette, right? A text message?* Ephra thought, and then shrugged. He was too eager to hear Ron's voice again. He typed in the number as carefully as he could in his excited state, then hit dial.

The phone was picked up almost immediately, but there was a clatter and a, "Fudge," and a "Hang on!"

Ephra hung on, legs jigging like mad.

"Gotcha!" Ron said with some effort. "Ephra? Is that you? Sorry, I dropped the phone in with Sticks."

"*Hi Ron*," Ephra said and, again, found that he was squeaking. He swallowed. "And good morning to Sticks, too. Tell her I'm sorry for invading her space."

Ron chuckled and the sound rolled through Ephra like a runaway train. *What I wouldn't give to have felt that laugh against my skin.*

"So … " Ron said, "How are you?"

Ephra slid over the arm of his chair and propped

his legs up on the back of the seat. "I'm very well, thank you." The words came out of him as a purr. "And you?"

"Good." Ephra could practically hear Ron blush. "Did you get your work done?"

"Yup, sent it off last night, and I've polished off the chapter for good measure."

"Cool." Ron paused. "You're free today, then?"

Ephra laughed softly. "I could be, if say, a tall man with tuggable curls might like to get a coffee."

"Shucks, I only drink tea," Ron teased.

"Damn, guess I'll have to sit here and write."

Ron hummed. "Of course, just because I only drink tea, doesn't mean I don't know where to get the best cup of coffee in London."

Ephra raised an eyebrow. "Now why would you know that?"

"Sometimes I need to take my clients out for a walk and a break."

"Ah, yes. I guess mediations must get tiring."

"They do, indeed." Ron let out a real huff. "But I cancelled my appointments for this afternoon. Sticks needs a day to bask before she gets back to work."

Ephra blinked, trying to figure out how Sticks could be involved in mediations. "Is she the alternative part?"

"Alternative … oh, my business card! Yes, she helps make sure people say only what they mean."

Ephra nodded. "I guess I can see how having a snake loose in the room might keep a person honest."

Ron let out another low laugh. "She is very good at her job. But we're off topic. I believe we were arranging an actual date?" It should have been a statement, but there was definitely a question mark at the end of his sentence.

"Yes, we were," Ephra affirmed. "So where is this coffee, then?"

There was a dull thud as Ron walked into something, followed by, "I'm okay!"

Ephra winced, but couldn't help grinning.

"Right, do you know where the sports centre is on my side of the bridge?"

"Yes, I know the place."

"Good." Ron paused thoughtfully. "Meet me there at, say, noon?"

Ephra looked at his clock. That would give him just enough time to pull his shit together. "That sounds like a plan."

Ron whispered something, assumedly to Sticks, then said, "I'm very much looking forward to this."

Ephra smiled. "Me too. It's been a while since I've been on a date, though, so you'll have to forgive me if I'm rusty."

"Don't worry. I'm, uh, in the same boat."

"Nice to know." Ephra clicked his tongue. "Well,

I'll see you, then?"

"Yes. See you," Ron said, clearly not wanting to hang up. Then suddenly he added, "Oh! Ephra, wear something you don't mind getting poop on."

"What?!" Ephra asked, but there was another thud and the phone disconnected.

Ephra lay blinking at his phone for a moment. He was mainly debating whether it was worth showering or not. *Where on Earth is he taking me that there's a risk I'm going to get covered in shit? And why would you take that risk on a first date?*

When Ephra eventually tried to get out of his chair again, he decided that a shower was not only worth it, but entirely necessary.

Ephra arrived outside the sports centre early. He had decided to dress in the only trainers and jeans he owned, topped with an old shirt and a sweatshirt that had frankly seen better days. The reason he was early was because he had changed this outfit four times over the course of the morning, and if he had to stay in the flat for a second longer, he would have inevitably changed again.

However, the moment he saw Ron, he wished he'd stuck with outfit number two, jeans and a smart jacket.

This was because Ron had clearly not listened to his own warning. He was wearing an actual Burberry coat, and what appeared to be those ridiculous Balenciaga sock shoes.

"Hello!" Ron said cheerily, and Ephra's wave of grumpiness almost completely subsided, but not quite.

"Hey," Ephra responded. "Is this what you call poop-ready clothing?"

Ron looked down at himself and seemed surprised by his own attire. "Oh, this is all gifted stuff. I can't stand wearing it normally, so I figured –"

"You'd get shit on a coat that's worth almost two grand?"

"Sugar! Is it worth that much?" Ron looked genuinely concerned. "I had no idea, I –"

Ephra suddenly leant up and kissed him on the cheek.

Ron twisted his lips. "What was that for?"

"Distraction," Ephra replied. "Sorry. I saw you walk up like that and felt self-conscious. I didn't mean to make you feel bad."

Ron cracked a smile and the sun came out from behind a cloud, giving him a genuine halo.

"Thank you," he said. "And for what it's worth, I like the rough and ready look on you." He took Ephra's hand and tugged. "Now come on, let's get the world's best coffee in you."

"The world's, hey? It's gone up in your estimation since our phone call."

Ron winked. "Maybe I've helped a few baristas meet their end since then."

"Oof, nothing like a bit of murder to get you ready for a first date."

"It was bracing!" Ron jested and opened the door to the sports centre.

It was then that Ephra realised that the sports centre was not just a convenient landmark to meet in front of, but was actually their destination. Inside was a bizarre mishmash of café and sports equipment shop. The walls were painted in that strange shade of blue that you only ever see in a leisure centre, but the café side of the room was heavily decorated with fake flowers and shabby-chic furniture.

"Go find a table," Ron said. "Something by the window. I'll order."

"Oh, okay, I'll have a –"

"Shush, let me guess!" Ron interjected. "If I'm wrong, I'll buy you another."

Ephra felt a little disconcerted, but nodded anyway. *Out of control again*, he thought, *and out of my comfort zone.*

He wandered across the room to a long wooden table next to the window. Through it, you could see the tennis courts. Two young women, around twenty, were going at it pretty hard. Ephra watched passively while he waited. Sports were not his thing.

"Nothing's really my thing," he grumbled to himself. He could feel his mood dropping like lead. *Maybe today wasn't a good day for this. Maybe I should have tried to get some more sleep.*

"Hey, are you okay?" Ron folded his great long legs over the bench seat opposite and rested the drinks tray to one side. "You look pale."

"Sorry," Ephra said. "I, uh, I'm suddenly not feeling so great."

Ron slid a hand across the table, palm up. He flexed his fingers. Ephra looked up at him. There, again, was that look of real concern, an expression of focused care and attention. Ephra placed his hand in Ron's. Ron smiled softly. "It's okay to not feel okay, okay?" He tilted his head. "Even on a first date."

Ephra mumbled something and started picking at the bench. Ron tugged at his fingers to draw his attention back. Ephra sighed. "I said that's easy to say when you're a sodding joyboat."

Ron laughed. "A joyboat?"

"Like a dreamboat, but chock full of happiness."

Ron pressed his teeth into his bottom lip. He was trying so hard not to laugh more than seemed appropriate that tears formed around his eyes. He took a deep breath and wiped his eyes clear, then said, "I know that's how I must seem to you, but we've known each other for what? Twenty-four hours? Joy is hard for me too, Ephra."

"Really?" Ephra asked, without a hint of sarcasm.

"You remember last night? In the gardens?"

Ephra nodded.

"Yes, well. I hate to think what I would have been like if you hadn't found Sticks." Ron paused and picked up his tea with his free hand. "I wasn't joking when I said Sticks is what makes my job feel worth it. What I do isn't easy, and joy is something I often find hard to fight for."

Ephra let out a breath he'd been holding as he listened. He sat up a little. "I get that," he said. "I'm used to living in this tight little bubble, and every time I try to expand the bubble something goes horribly wrong so … I guess, I guess I'm being a bit of a dick." He smiled coyly at Ron as he said it, so he'd know he wasn't trying to be self-deprecating.

Ron laced his fingers through Ephra's. "Absolutely. I mean, what kind of man lets the world's best coffee get cold?" He gestured to the tray.

Ephra felt a wave of relief wash over him and, happy to change the subject, he moved the mug from the tray to the table and slid it towards himself. It was a latte, a good choice. Normally he drank cappuccinos, but then normally the coffee he drank was terrible, so it was worth trying. As he brought the drink to his mouth he saw Ron's facial expression – full of wonder and anticipation – and he snorted the foam right over the edge of the cup.

He put the drink down quickly and grabbed a napkin, still spluttering.

"What?! What is it?"

"Your face, you bloody fool," Ephra said, wiping his mouth, then the table. "You looked like a kid about to blow out his birthday candles." He laughed.

When he caught his breath, Ron was grinning at him. "I love that noise," he said. Ephra's pulse quickened. Ron pressed his lips to their still clasped hands. "Go on, try again. I'll watch the tennis this time, I promise," he added.

Ron turned his face to the window, unknotting their hands, and Ephra paused to take in how stupidly handsome Ron was in profile. Then he picked up the latte and took a sip.

It was lovely. It was smooth and creamy and rich and exactly like you hope coffee will be when you smell it, but never is.

"Fuck me," Ephra breathed. "Why is this so *good*?"

Ron beamed. "Can I look at you now?"

"Yes, please do, I need you to explain this godly creation."

Ron snapped his face back round. "It's great, isn't it?"

"Yes, yes! But *how?*" Ephra asked, taking another sip. "I didn't think coffee could be *this.*"

"Well, let's just say a feather-footed friend told me where to get the best coffee imaginable, and now I pay to have it used here, so that I have access whenever a client goes off the rails."

"Ah!" Ephra said. "So it's *expensive.*"

Ron lowered his brow, but he was still smiling. "Actually, it's the same price as most blends you'd get in a chain."

Ephra looked sceptical.

"It is! I swear. But, of course, I get the beans blessed by my guru immediately before it's brewed." Ron's face was so perfectly deadpan that Ephra almost thought he was serious. Then a wicked smile snuck across his face and Ephra laughed again.

"You had me going for a minute there."

Ron jostled his curls back and forth. "I can be self-aware when I want to be."

Ephra suddenly spotted a fleck of foam in Ron's hair. He reached across the table and pinched it with his fingers. "Foam," he explained at Ron's slack-jawed expression. "I thought I'd get rid of it before we get covered in excrement."

"Thanks," Ron said. "I hate getting bits in it."

"You're not going to explain the poop thing, then?"

Ron's nose scrunched happily. "Nope."

"Why not?"

"Because. You've lived around here for a while now, and should know what we're going to do. And if you don't, then I want it to be a surprise."

Ephra's stomach twinged. "You should know I'm not great at not being in control."

Ron nodded. "I am beginning to get that impression, but if you don't like it, we'll leave immediately."

"Alright."

When they were done with their drinks, Ephra bought them another round to go. Ron had wanted to pay, but Ephra scowled at him, gave him a peck on the cheek and said, "Don't you bloody dare."

Cups in hand, they made their way north and into Kensington Gardens, back along the path they'd taken the day before to the Peter Pan statue. This time, however, they didn't quite make it to Peter. Ron caught Ephra's hand a few metres before the fence started, and dragged him off into the trees. There were a couple of tourists standing around with their arms out, holding what appeared to be bits of apple. Ron dodged away from them into a smaller cluster of trees. The golden canopy erupted with chirping as they ducked under the branches.

When Ephra could stand again, he found himself in a small clearing, surrounded by dozens of bright green parakeets. They bounced excitedly on their branches, waiting to be fed. Ephra watched them dance about with awe.

"Do you like it?" Ron asked.

Ephra held out a hand, and one of the birds leapt onto him. "I very much like this," he said in a breathy voice. He turned to Ron. "How did you know I like birds?"

Ron's face lit up. "I didn't, I just really like coming here. I don't feed them because the park tells you not to, but they're so friendly."

"That they are. You're very friendly, aren't you, girlie?" The little bird chirped on his finger and suddenly there was a flurry of feathers.

The next thing Ephra knew, there was a parakeet sat on every available perch-point on his body. Ephra turned to face Ron, who was clearly just as shocked at this behaviour as Ephra was. They exchanged a look of utter surprise, and then Ephra began to shake with laughter. Ron cackled.

"Okay, birdies, you're all very friendly, wonderful little chaps." Ephra laughed. "But you know we don't have any food, don't you? Ron here said we're not supposed to feed you."

There was a lot of tweeting and hopping, but they all stayed where they were, being very attentive to the sound of Ephra's voice.

"Hmm … it looks like they like you as much as I do," Ron said.

Ephra felt blood rush to his face. "Oh, I don't know about that. These birds seem to like me a hell of a lot, don't you? Chirp, chirp."

The parakeets all replied, "Chirp, chirp," in unison.

Ephra stared at the little green creatures on his arms. *Surely, that's not normal*, he thought.

When he looked at Ron, the man appeared to be somewhat flabbergasted. He licked his lips nervously and said, "You know, my mother once told me that folks who spoke the language of birds were incredibly wise."

Ephra chuckled. "I'd love to take that compliment, but I can't actually talk to them. I think they just like the sound of my voice."

Ron moved towards Ephra and placed a hand on his waist. He turned him gently to face the tree behind.

"Looks like they understand you well enough." Ron pointed.

All of the parakeets in the tree were focused on Ephra, turning their little heads this way and that to get a better look at him. Ephra's jaw dropped. *That's* definitely *not normal.*

Ephra felt the birds on his head hop down onto his shoulders. Ron's arms slipped around his waist, and he popped his head on top of Ephra's. "You must be a very old soul," he whispered.

Ephra snorted. "Well, that's something we can agree on. You should have heard the noise I made getting out of my chair this morning."

A sound, somewhere between mirth and music, rumbled through Ron's body. Ephra felt every inch of it and shivered. He wanted nothing more than to turn and kiss him right then, but he was very aware he was still covered in parakeets.

He cleared his throat and said (not thinking it would actually work), "Hey, good little birds. Do you mind popping back into the tree a minute?" He raised his arms. Ron lifted his head. They both watched as the birds politely took flight and landed amongst the branches. "Huh," Ephra said. "They must know arms up means get off, or something."

He put his arms down and placed his hands over Ron's where they held him.

"I do, by the way," Ron murmured into Ephra's black locks.

"You do what?"

"I do like you as much as these parakeets do. *More,* even." There was a growl to his voice.

Ephra turned his head slightly and shifted his

weight, trying to see Ron's face. When their eyes met, Ephra couldn't help but notice that the greys and blues of Ron's irises seemed to sparkle in the light, like the peaks of waves on a rolling ocean.

"How are you real?" Ephra asked.

Ron laughed in response, and that was as much as Ephra could take. He spun and pulled Ron's face down to his level. Ron didn't stop laughing, even when Ephra pressed their lips together and twisted his fingers into his hair. Instead, Ron placed a hand in the centre of Ephra's lower back, supporting him as he stretched. His other hand found its way under the layers of Ephra's jumper and shirt to his hip. The cold chill of Ron's frozen fingers against his skin made Ephra gasp, "*Fuck me!*"

Ron cackled. "Not in front of your bird friends."

Ephra grunted at him and nudged his nose in annoyance. He pushed himself free of Ron's arms and offered a finger to one of the parakeets as he began to walk away.

"You know, for a man who doesn't swear, that guy has a really dirty mind," Ephra said to the bird, trying to mask his panting breath.

There was a laugh behind him.

"He also has a really dirty laugh." Ephra paused at the tree line. "That being said, I hope he knows I like him just as much."

The parakeet chirped. Ephra turned slightly

towards Ron, but continued talking to his avian pal. "Yes. You're right. Joy does seem a lot easier when he's around."

The bird fluttered off his finger and Ephra ducked under the tree line, knowing Ron would follow him.

For some reason, the moment they reached the top of the street Ephra burst into a sprint and yelled, "Race you!"

Ron very happily gave chase, catching up with ease due to his enormous gait. Fearing Ron might win, Ephra stopped abruptly on the bottom step in front of the townhouse. He planted a hand in the centre of Ron's chest and kissed him deeply. It almost sent Ephra spinning, but before his head began to whirl too much he pulled away and bolted up to the door.

Ron took the last few steps slowly, seemingly defeated. However, when he reached the top step, he loomed over Ephra, pressing him back into the door.

"You cheated," he whispered, a smile on his lips – lips that were so close. Ephra braced himself, closing his eyes and taking in the spiced scent of Ron's skin.

Then Ephra heard the key slide into the lock and suddenly he was falling backwards. Ron caught him quickly, grinning. He pecked Ephra on the forehead and stood him upright. "Tea?" he asked.

"Coffee," Ephra grumbled, following Ron into the living room. His feigned ill temper slid away as he noticed how tidy the room was. "I thought you only cleaned for clients?" he said, hoping Ron hadn't done it for him.

"Sticks told me I had to!" Ron yelled, continuing on into his kitchen.

Ephra eyed the snake in her tank. She raised her head, returning his stare.

"She did?" Ephra asked, taking a seat.

"Yes! She said falling over twice in one phone call was unacceptable, and I really need to get my sh-sugar together."

"I guess she said 'shit'?"

"Yes."

"Well, she's very eloquent for a snake. But, I don't know. I kind of liked the book piles."

There was a hiss of hot water, a chink of metal on china, and then Ron returned to the living room carrying two mugs. "I liked the piles too, they made good side tables. But Sticks gets what Sticks wants."

"Is that so?" Ephra said in Sticks' direction. Her head bobbed, then she stretched along the length of her tank, basking under her heat lamp. Ephra huffed.

"You know, I'm sensing that maybe there's still some animosity between the two of you," Ron declared, planting the mugs on the table and slapping his legs. "I'm afraid I simply can't have that."

"I wouldn't call it animosity," Ephra replied. "I just, I can't get rid of the image of this gigantic snake I thought I saw in the dark yesterday."

"I think it would help if you got to know her, don't you?"

Ephra looked at him like he'd gone mad. "She's a snake, Ron."

"And your friends in the park were birds, Ephra."

"That's different." Ephra crossed his arms.

"How?" Ron mimicked his pose, which irritated Ephra so much and so unexpectedly that he immediately uncrossed his arms again without meaning to.

"Birds can't kill you!" Ephra said with genuine frustration.

"You've clearly never watched a Hitchcock movie."

"Yes, I have, and it was all lies."

Ron laughed and took Ephra's hand. Ephra rolled his eyes, but let himself be pulled up from the sofa, over to the tank. Once there, Ron let him go and reached down into the tank to pick up Sticks. She wrapped herself with grace and ease around Ron's right arm, allowing him to support the majority of her body with his left. Comfortable, Sticks raised her head to look at Ephra.

"She likes it when I pet her head. Give it a try," Ron suggested. Ephra looked at him doubtfully. "She's not venomous, and she very rarely bites."

"She bites?!"

"Only when she's hungry, and I promise, she's been well fed since I got her home."

Ephra took a deep breath, then reached a shaky hand toward Sticks' head. Very, very carefully, he ran the tips of his fingers over her scales. They were surprisingly smooth. Her speckled surface gave the impression of gravel, so Ephra had expected her to feel like sandpaper. He relaxed a bit and stroked her again. Sticks turned her head into his palm and tickled it with her tongue. Ephra jumped, then chuckled. Something glinted in the snake's eyes. It looked an awful lot like amusement.

"Is it me, or is she smiling?" Ephra asked.

Ron grinned. "She likes you. Oh, Sticks, no!"

Sticks very quickly wrapped herself around Ephra's wrist and slithered up his arm. "Whoa, whoa! Ron! What is she doing?"

Ron grimaced. "She really does actually like you, Ephra. I thought she was just cold the other night when she slid onto you, but I think she has a genuine thing for you."

"Are you only saying that to try and make me feel calmer about your snake trying to eat me?" Ephra panted, the image of giant grey-silver eyes flashing through his mind.

"She is not trying to eat you, Ephra." Ron pressed his hand against Ephra's chest. "Take a deep breath. I promise you, she's not going to hurt you. Are you, Sticks?"

Ephra chanced a look at the snake's head just in time to see her roll her spine, as if to shrug. Ephra blinked.

"Come on, Sticks. I think Ephra's had enough of your antics for one day." Ron took Ephra's wrist again and the snake obediently crawled off Ephra's shoulders. Ron placed her gently back in the tank, then turned to Ephra. "You okay?"

Ephra took a deep breath. "Yeah, yes. I think I am, actually." He leant over the edge of the tank and petted Sticks' head again. "Yes, okay, Sticks. I'll make you a deal: no more surprises like that, and I promise I'll pet you like this every time I visit."

Sticks looked at him, then flicked her tongue against his palm again, like she was shaking hands. Out of the corner of his eye, Ephra thought he saw something flicker in Sticks' water dish, but Ron's arms slipped around his waist and the sensation made Ephra close his eyes before he could get a good look.

"You should be careful what promises you make in front of her," Ron whispered in his ear. "She doesn't like it when you break them."

"I'll bear that in mind," Ephra answered.

Ron rocked them both gently backwards away from the tank, then spun Ephra round and led him over to the sofa. They spent the rest of the afternoon letting their beverages go cold.

The rest of the week went surprisingly smoothly. Ephra would shake off his restless night's sleep, sit and write in the flat during office hours, then rush off at five to meet Ron somewhere. More often than not, they would end their date with a walk through the park and a longing kiss under the bridge where they had to part.

When he was alone, Ephra would sort through his feelings, trying to poke a hole in something, find the snag that might cause everything to unravel. But there really wasn't anything. Since their first date, Ron had gone out of his way to make sure Ephra had equal say. They alternated deciding where to go, and Ron regularly checked in with Ephra, making sure he was on board with his schemes. One night had involved a picnic on the steps next to the Albert Memorial, followed by a show at the Royal Albert Hall. Ephra had never really been one for theatre, but he enjoyed how Ron squeezed his hand in the tense scenes, lifted his long legs when he laughed at the comedy, and rested his head on him as the play drew to a close.

Before Ephra knew it, it was Friday morning, and he actually had three chapters of his next novel to send to Halwyn. He sent them at 9AM on the dot, and decided that he'd take the rest of the day slowly. If he got some more work done, great; if he didn't, three chapters would be more than enough to satiate his over-saturated publisher.

He made himself some pancakes, figuring he'd better get back in practice, in case he had to make someone breakfast in the near future. Then he took a shower. Ephra had just pulled his trousers on when there was a knock at his door.

He wandered out of the bedroom, bare-chested, shirt in hand. When he looked through the spyhole, all he could see was a blur of pink. Ephra braced himself, then opened the door.

"Halwyn, what are you doing here?"

Halwyn Tân was stood in the hallway holding an enormous gift basket wrapped in shimmering pink cellophane. He used it like a battering ram as he entered, and sang, "Morning, Money-maker! Could you direct me to a table, this thing is difficult to navigate with."

Ephra jumped out of the way quickly as Halwyn walked straight into his kitchen. He winced as he caught sight of Halwyn's suit of the day, which was an eye-watering fluorescent pink. "The table is exactly where it's always been, Hal," Ephra said through gritted teeth. "And you still haven't answered my question!"

Halwyn let out a deep laugh. To Ephra's ears it sounded menacing, but then Ephra thought everything Halwyn did was somewhat evil.

"I came to bring you this gift basket, silly," Halwyn explained. "And I wanted to thank you for the extra chapter."

Ephra propped himself against the kitchen door frame as Halwyn placed the basket on the table. "Did your phone and your personal courier die on the same day?"

Halwyn turned. There was a momentary flash of annoyance across his face, quickly replaced by amusement. "No, they didn't," he said plainly. "But if I didn't drop by every now and then, I'd miss this wondrous gun show." He wafted his hand up and down, gesturing at Ephra's naked upper body.

Ephra huffed and quickly shoved his arms into his shirt and began to work his way through the buttons. "What's this really about?"

Halwyn sucked at his bottom lip. It sounded like he was grappling with how to broach his real intent, but Ephra was fairly convinced he was watching him do up his shirt.

When Ephra straightened up, Halwyn was playing with the pearlescent ribbon on the basket. "I suppose I just wanted to discuss this new-found enthusiasm you have for writing romance."

Ephra folded his arms. "Why, is there a problem?"

"No, no!" Halwyn started. "But I wanted to see if there's anything the publishing company, or indeed I myself, can do to keep this burst of inspiration going."

Ephra actually laughed so hard he had to press one palm to the wall to keep his balance. "I'm fine, thank you, Halwyn," he said once he was stable.

"Have you found a little romance of your own, perhaps?" Halwyn was studying Ephra's face, and it was very disconcerting.

"For the second time this week, Hal, my personal life is none of your business."

"So you have?" Hal raised an eyebrow. "And nothing bad has happened yet? He's not stood you up or died suddenly? It's all going smoothly?"

Ephra's jaw stiffened. "You're over-stepping, Hal."

"I'm sorry, Ephra. It's just that I remember all the phone calls, the sobbing. You don't have the best track record and I am your *only* friend." The words fell from Halwyn's mouth with such syrup, it made Ephra's nose wrinkle in disgust.

"Believe it or not, Halwyn, there is more to my life than you and that chum bucket you call a publishing house," Ephra snarled.

Halwyn raised his hands. "Wow, Ephra, okay. Message received." He smiled falsely. "I guess I should congratulate you, though. I am happy for you. Even if things will inevitably fall apart, leaving me to pick up the pieces of your fragile ego. After all, we *love* love, no matter how short-lived."

Ephra's skin tingled like it was on fire. He took a step backward and pointed to the front door. "Get out, Halwyn."

"Sure thing."

After Halwyn left, Ephra fidgeted around his flat for about an hour, trying to calm down. He then reached a point where it felt like, if he didn't voluntarily leave the flat, his body was going to vibrate him through the walls. He threw on his wool coat and ploughed his way out of the building.

He felt better the moment the cold air hit his skin, but as soon as he let himself think again his head filled with the image of Halwyn Tân's sickening smile. The rage returned, spiralling upwards swiftly, until he found himself yelling over Long Water, "*Fucking piece of shit!*"

Birds in nearby trees took flight, and Ephra felt a

little pang of guilt. "Sorry," he whispered after them.

A bird in the bush nearest to him chirped.

"Don't start that again," Ephra said. "I already feel like I'm going crazy."

Silence. Ephra smiled and held back a thank you.

He marched on along the river, thinking he'd get himself a nice coffee and have a sit outside, and somewhere in the midst of it all Halwyn's smug face would fuck off out of his head. However, when the turning that led up to the bridge and the sports centre came, he walked straight past it. In fact, he walked himself straight to Ron's house.

As Ephra put his foot on the first step up to the building, the door sprang open.

"Thank you, ladies. It's been a pleasure, as always," Ron said cheerily. "And remember, the pair of you, what you say in front of Sticks can't be taken back!"

Two women appeared in the doorway behind him. One wore neutral-coloured exercise wear, and had a warm, motherly smile. The other wore a pristine blue dress, fringed with what appeared to be real peacock feathers. The former gave Ron a hug before trotting down the steps. When she saw Ephra she gave him a little wave and a nod, as you might do with a neighbour, and then she jogged up the street and out of sight.

Peacock lady, however, stopped in the doorway and muttered something to Ron.

"No, Mrs Z, you know the rules. Once you've made the verbal agreement you can't rescind it, or well, I don't have to tell *you* the consequences," Ron replied.

The woman scoffed and elegantly swished past him. She paused again when she noticed Ephra, and studied his face as if she recognised him.

"Do I know you?" Ephra asked.

A smile hooked the corner of 'Mrs Z's' pursed lips. She looked back at Ron over her shoulder and said, "You ought to be careful with this one. He seems the type who doesn't like to be tied down." She let out a sharp laugh and then sashayed off down the road to a black street car.

Ron peered down at Ephra. Ephra could see the cogs whirring, trying to figure out what the woman had meant. Then he shrugged, and his normal steadfast grin reappeared. "Hello, glum-bum, what brings you here?"

Ephra tilted his head. "Did you just call me glum-bum?"

Ron laughed. "Well, you are stood on my bottom step looking like someone stole all your sunshine."

Ephra rocked backwards and forwards on his heels. "Yeah … I, uh, I don't really know why I'm here. I-I had a bit of a fight with my publisher. It got personal and … " Ephra stopped himself short of saying something stupid.

"Well, you're in luck. Those two ladies were my only appointment this afternoon. Come on." Ron wiggled an outstretched hand at Ephra.

Ephra hesitated. If he went inside, he'd have to tell Ron what Halwyn had said, and that meant explaining what he meant. Ephra didn't know how to explain that Halwyn was right: that beyond Ron, Halwyn was the only person in Ephra's life who came close to resembling a 'friend'. *How do I explain that my only friend is someone who makes my life hell?*

Ephra's mind spiralled downward so quickly, he didn't realise the tears were forming until Ron came stumbling down the steps and enveloped him in his arms. They stood there silently for a little while, Ephra's face pressed lightly to Ron's chest. Something about the warmth and the dark and the scent of Ron's skin prevented Ephra from having a full breakdown.

Eventually, Ephra whispered, "Okay. I'm okay."

Ron kissed the top of his head and stepped back, giving his arms a squeeze. "Are you sure?"

Ephra shrugged. "I'll make it inside the house."

Ron smiled softly. He put an arm around Ephra's shoulders and coaxed him up the stairs. Inside, Ephra threw his coat on the floor, kicked his shoes after it and slumped into the living room. He thought Ron would follow, but when he turned, Ron was tucking his coat away in the hall cupboard.

"I'm sorry," Ephra said.

Ron hung the coat on the rail and then walked over. He kissed Ephra's head again. "No need to be sorry.

Come over here." Ron wandered over to the sofa and pointed. "Lie down."

Ephra did as he was told. Ron pulled a blanket from some magic hole and spread it over Ephra's body, then he pushed the coffee table back and sat cross-legged on the floor. He tucked his hand under the blanket to find Ephra's and gave it a squeeze. "You don't have to tell me what that was about if you don't want to," he whispered. "But I promise I won't judge if you do."

Ephra licked the inside of his mouth, turning his face into the sofa cushion. He worked his thumb over Ron's forefinger, noticing the bump of each joint, the rough callus on the pad. When he was fairly certain he could sketch Ron's forefinger from the memory of its shape alone, he turned back to him and said, "It's a long story."

"All the important ones are."

Ephra breathed, taking in Ron's golden complexion. He fixed his gaze on the scruff of stubble along his chin and began, "Halwyn, my publisher, he's the one that drags me up off the floor. He did it the first time I met him, and he's done it every time since. Every time I thought I was in love, but got my heartbroken ... "

"Well that's –"

"I hate him," Ephra said firmly, before Ron could finish his sentence. "He doesn't do it to be kind; he doesn't do it because he likes me. He does it because I make him a lot of money, so it's best to keep me running."

"I'm sure that's not true."

"I'm sure it is." Ephra felt his chest tighten. "I sent him three chapters today, more than he'd asked for, and he came to the flat, barged right in. He said he wanted to discuss my enthusiasm, but what he wanted to get at was you. I told him to stop, to leave it, and then he …"

"He what?"

"He *reminded* me that he is my only friend and that whatever is happening between you and I will 'inevitably' end." Ephra could feel the sting of tears in his eyes again.

Ron used his free hand to pull Ephra's un-styled hair back from his face, and rested his chin on the sofa. "He shouldn't have said that to you, Ephra. You're right to be upset."

At the sound of those words, Ephra shuddered. A wave of relief and sorrow rolled through his body. Tears streaked down his cheeks. "I – I know I can be an arsehole to him. Even today … but he pulls at my strings, brings up things I've tried to forget, pokes and prods, and I see it and it … " Ephra shook again.

"It hurts," Ron finished his sentence.

Ephra nodded, eyes still closed. Ron ran a rough thumb across Ephra's cheeks to wipe away the escaped tears.

"Can I make something very clear, Ephra?" Ron asked, gently. When Ephra didn't respond he added, "I'm going to need you to open those beautiful brown eyes of yours and say yes."

Ephra took a deep breath and pulled his eyes open. A few rogue tears fell, but Ron cleaned them up again. Ephra waited for him to finish and then said, "Yes."

Ron looked very serious. He looked over at Sticks' tank, then back at Ephra, "I swear to you, I have no intention of letting this end any time soon, if that's okay with you, of course."

"Why?" Ephra said without meaning to. "I'm a mess and a grump and –"

"And you're honest, and you're kind, and you humour me with all my weirdness –"

"You're not weird. You look like a bloody demi-god," Ephra snapped.

Ron let out a short bark of laughter, then he shook his head and continued, "You're patient, you're brave, you're sensitive and quite frankly, I love that you're all that and that you're a grump."

"And a mess?"

"And a mess," Ron confirmed.

"But why?" Ephra said again.

Ron shrugged. He sat back a little, taking in the white ceiling and the earthy walls. "I spend every afternoon in this room with Sticks listening to people squabble over trivial little things. I stick my oar in when I can, try and steer the conversation, and eventually an agreement is reached and my clients leave."

"And?"

"And then they come back and have the same argument over something new and I know that nothing I do really matters to them, because all they want to do is pick a fight." Ron took a breath. "It's like I'm a ghost, like I'm not here, like I'm ferrying them around and around in circles. And when I'm done for the day, I put away my smile, I don't tidy up and I forget to feed myself." He wagged his finger. "I didn't even really leave the house unless Sticks got out and then, boom, there you were."

"Me?"

"You, Ephra." Ron swallowed and Ephra could feel a little tremor running up Ron's arm into the hand he was holding. "You saw me, and I didn't feel like a ghost anymore. This grumpy, sweet, sarcastic guy spent his whole day helping me find a snake in a ridiculously large park, got the fright of his life, and at the end of it told me that I'd made him laugh more than he had in a long time. I didn't feel pointless anymore, Ephra, I felt seen. You make me feel seen."

Ephra shuffled out of the blanket a bit. He sat himself up and placed a foot either side of Ron's hips, then let go of Ron's hand and pulled his golden head towards him. "Thank you, joyboat."

Ron snorted against Ephra's shoulder.

"For the record, I don't want this to end any time soon, either."

"Good," said Ron. "Because I did swear it in front of Sticks, and like I said, she's a stickler for promises."

Ephra tilted his head to look at the tank. Sticks had her head raised, looking at him expectantly. Ephra smiled. "You better hold him to it."

Sticks put her head down and slithered out of sight.

The next morning Ephra woke up in an unfamiliar bed, and frankly, he was quite happy about it. The mattress was hard enough to support, but soft enough to cradle. The sheets were silky against his skin and smelt fresh as a daisy. The brief moment of confusion regarding his whereabouts was promptly shoved away by the picture on the bedside table: Ron stood in front of his townhouse with Sticks draped around his neck. Her tongue was flicking his cheek, causing him to squint and laugh.

Ephra let out a warm hum and spread himself out flat in the bed. After their talk, Ron and he had cuddled up together on the sofa and watched some rubbish on TV, made dinner in Ron's over-sized kitchen filled with ridiculous gadgets (Ephra had been bemused by the lack of kettle until he'd discovered Ron's instant boiling water tap), and then Ron had insisted Ephra stay the night and use one of the guest beds.

"I want to make sure you actually sleep," he'd said. "I get the impression it's a rare event."

Ephra had grumbled, "I'll sleep when I'm dead."

"My family's going to love you."

Ron'd given him a set of loose-fitting pyjama bottoms and packed him off with a cup of hot chocolate. Ephra had sat on the edge of the bed and brooded over the cup of sweet steaming milk for a while, but the moment his head hit the pillow, he'd been out cold.

That's probably the best I've ever slept, Ephra thought with joyful surprise. *That's probably the best anyone's ever slept.*

He smiled at the ceiling, delighting in the fact that he was, for once, well-rested. He didn't quite want to get up yet, but Ephra was eager to see Ron. In the end he compromised. He pulled the fleece blanket off the top of the bedspread and wrapped it around himself like a shawl. This way he could still sort of be in bed and see Ron.

He wandered out onto the landing, counting the number of doors. There were three on the first floor, but Ephra knew there were two floors above him.

How does anyone afford to live like this? passed

through his mind, but he didn't really care. Between Ron's naivety about the cost of things and the couple of times Ron had spoken about his family, Ephra had surmised that Ron was from an affluent background and he didn't feel right about asking anything further. Not yet, anyway.

Ephra reached the stairs and listened for signs of life, trying to guess whether Ron was up or down. A delightful hum drifted up from the living room, followed by a, "Stay right there, I just need to change your water dish."

Ephra padded down the steps carefully.

"Yes, Sticks, I'll remind him when he wakes up. He knows a promise is a promise."

Ephra grinned as he entered the room where Ron was in the process of clearing out Sticks' tank. "You two talking about me? My ears are burning."

Ron glanced up, barely managing to keep hold of the huge ceramic dish in his hands. "Oh, yes! Sticks was complaining that you still haven't petted her yet."

Ephra laughed. "Where is she? I'll do it now."

Ron looked awkwardly around the room. "She's here somewhere," he murmured.

"She's not in the tank?" Ephra's heart skipped.

Ron pulled a face. "No … I take her out to clean it, but she'll be around. Sticks, come out. You promised no more surprises!"

There was a loud hiss and Sticks appeared from under the sofa. Ephra breathed. He didn't know why it was such a relief to know where she was, despite the fact she was out of her tank and still very mobile. It just made him significantly calmer to be able to see her. He strutted across the room in his blanket and took a seat, then patted his lap. Sticks looked at him in confusion. Ephra thought, if she could talk, Sticks probably would have said, "Do I look like a dog to you?"

"Come on! If you come up here, I can scratch your head until Ron's done with your tank," Ephra explained.

When that didn't work, he leant awkwardly towards the ground and offered his hand for her to slither up. Sticks practically punched his palm with her nose.

"Okay, you want to stay down there, do you? Hang on." Ephra lay down on the sofa, rolled onto his stomach and began scratching Sticks' head. "There. Happy?"

There was a dull thud as Ron dropped the water dish back into Sticks' tank. "You seem like you're in a good mood today," he said. "Did you sleep well?"

"Better than I have in yonks." Ephra leant up a little, so he could see Ron's face. "Thanks for making me stay. I think I just would have sat staring at Halwyn's stupid gift basket all night if I'd gone home." Even saying Halwyn's name made Ephra's stomach churn.

"It's no problem. You're always welcome here."

"Thanks," Ephra grinned. Then he thought about the prospect of going home, and the possibility that Halwyn might turn up unannounced again.

"What are you trundling over in that head of yours?" Ron plucked a cloth from the coffee table and ran it through his hands.

Ephra let out a sigh. "Honestly? I'm dreading going home, being somewhere certain putrid publishers can find me."

"Ah." Ron squatted down at the end of the sofa and scuffed his nose against Ephra's. "Well, when I said you're welcome here, I did mean it. I don't mind you using my house as a hideout."

"Really?" Ephra's eyebrows flailed in surprise. "Are you sure? I mean, obviously I'd try to be a good house guest, but I'd probably end up writing at all sorts of odd hours, and I can be horrendously grumpy."

"Yes, of course, I'm sure." Ron chuckled and pecked him on the cheek. "I wouldn't suggest it otherwise. And it's not like we'll be tripping over each other in this place." He hummed, blushing a little. "At least, I'll try not to trip over you."

"And I'll try not to knock you off your feet." Ephra winked, then added, "Whoops, too late!" as Ron laughed, lost his balance and fell onto his backside.

Ron covered his face with his hand. "One day I'll be graceful," he said, then flipped his hair out of his face and pulled himself up to his feet in a movement that Ephra couldn't help but compare to that of a wave collapsing upward into the side of a cliff. "Oh, I should warn you before I forget! I've had an emergency booking for 1PM, so you'll need to make yourself scarce for a little while this afternoon."

Ephra let out a groan. "I guess I should go home and get some things … I can't wear the same clothes forever." His arm was beginning to ache from hanging awkwardly off the edge of the sofa, so he gave Sticks one last good scratch and sat up. He twisted his lips thoughtfully. "Do you think you could mediate me out of my publishing contract some time?"

Ron chuckled, stepping over Sticks to sit down next to him. "I'm afraid that's not really the sort of thing I do."

"I thought mediators helped folks work through arguments?"

Ron wrapped an arm around him and rested his head on Ephra's shoulder. "We do, but I don't deal with legal cases, only personal disagreements. I don't really have the expertise to help you with that Dip Dab you work with."

"Dick?" Ephra asked.

"That's the one."

Ephra laughed and kissed him. "I love how, even when you're giving me bad news, you can make me laugh."

Ron grinned. "And I love that you listen well enough to understand my swear words."

Ephra pressed his face into Ron's mountain of curls for a moment and chuckled. *I could listen to you swear for an eternity*, he thought, but he didn't say it, because who said stuff like that less than a week after meeting someone?

Eventually, Ephra reformed his line of thought and said, "I guess I'll have to write my way out of this contract, then."

Ron squeezed his side. "You'll be alright, okay? I'm not going anywhere, and I'll say that as many times as you need to hear. No bother, no questions."

Ephra breathed calmly, eyes closed, and whispered, "Bless that bird that steered me to you."

"What did you say?" Ron asked.

"Nothing, just, I still can't believe you're real."

Ephra didn't spend long in his flat. He packed a bag with lightning speed, retrieved his laptop, and spat at the pink cellophane blob on his kitchen table. Then he left again. It was hard to feel sad about running away from a home full of nightmares and bad memories. And he had to admit he was more than a little excited to stay with Ron.

Ron had told him he could use his house as a hideout, so he would. Ephra would hide where Halwyn couldn't find him, write his novel, and be done with the whole damn thing. And, as a bonus, he'd get to see Ron's sunshine smile every day.

On the way home through the park, he began to daydream about all the other jobs he might try once his publishing deal was done and dusted. Nothing entry level ever really paid enough in London, but he had transferable skills. He could be an administrator, or a copywriter. Working in an office would make a nice change to being tucked away in his musty living room all day.

On the other hand, though, he wasn't quite sure if he'd manage a regular nine-to-five. He'd become so accustomed to working at night that he wondered how he ever saw daylight. Maybe he'd be better off working some kind of night shift, but what kind of night jobs needed his skillset?

Feeling the spiral, Ephra shook himself. He took in the glass-like surface of the Serpentine, the sound of the birds in the trees, the crunch of the fresh leaf fall under his feet. Honestly, it didn't matter what he ended up doing for work. As long as Halwyn Tân had nothing to do with it, he was sure he'd love it. And, until then, well, he was actually rather amusing himself with his current romance project.

After a week staying at Ron's, Ephra sent Halwyn another three chapters, in which his couple accidentally got locked into a museum at night and ended up having an intense, moonlit picnic in the main hall. There were confessions of love, throes of passion, running from security. It had it all.

Within an hour of him sending the pages, Halwyn phoned. Ron peered at Ephra over a pulp fiction novel and said, "You should probably answer it, shouldn't you?"

Ephra gnawed at his lip. "I don't know that I've got the strength to deal with him."

"You do." Ron winked. "I know you can move mountains, Ephra. So take a deep breath and give this particular mountain a quick shove off a sharp cliff."

Ephra sighed and picked up his phone. He went into the hall to take the call, perching himself on the bottom of the stairs.

"Yes, Halwyn?" he said.

There was a momentary pause, then Halwyn began in his normal overly-cheery voice, "Ephra, my dear, I thought you were dead! How are you?"

"I'm fine."

Another pause. "Well, I calling about those chapters you just sent. Thank you for them by the way, it's so refreshing not to have to squeeze you like a …"

"Stone?" Ephra suggested.

Halwyn cackled. "Oh, exactly! Very good." He coughed. "I have to say, though, I am getting a little bit concerned about the quality of your work."

"*Excuse me?*"

"Yes, well, I didn't want to say anything before, early days, you know. But now I've got six chapters in front of me, I'm a bit concerned about the prose … and the plot, if I'm honest. I mean, your heroine isn't exactly aspirational, is she? She's a bit depressing, with all her umming and ahing over whether she really deserves this man who so clearly likes her." Halwyn took a breath. "And to be honest, I'm not really sure I understand why your hero likes her. He's such a breath of fresh air, and she's the verbal equivalent of a knee to the knackers."

Ephra stood up, his fists clenched with anger. "You've changed your tune since the last time I saw you. You thought my first chapters were great last week."

"I said I could see your enthusiasm; I never said the work was good."

Ephra's brain froze into a white hot blur of rage. He closed his eyes, held the phone away from his face, and let a growl rumble through his body. *Mother fudger.*

When he was done, he pressed the phone back to his ear and said, "So what? You want me to go back through and re-write everything?"

"Would you?" Hal said. "That would be wonderful, Ephra. And do try and find some of that brooding bad-boy energy you normally work with. All this happiness and doubt is giving me a migraine. It really is awful to read."

Ephra snarled. "Yes, of course."

"Great, I look forward to the redraft by the end of next week!" Halwyn sang.

Ephra hung up and stood rigidly in the middle of Ron's hallway. A few seconds later, a gentle hand took the phone from him, and he was wrapped into a tight embrace.

"I just want out," Ephra whispered. "I feel like I'm suffocating."

Ron combed his fingers through Ephra's hair and looked deeply into his eyes. "One more book, one more push, then you're free. And I am not going anywhere."

That afternoon, Ron had another client. He'd offered to cancel, but Ephra said it would do him some good to go for a walk, get a coffee, be out in the world. Ron had insisted on making him up a flask, though, so fifteen minutes before the session, Ephra headed out of the townhouse in his big wool coat with a thermos the size of his head.

At least, if anyone comes at me, I have a nice sturdy weapon, Ephra thought.

Automatically, he walked towards the park. There wasn't really any question of where he would end up. For the past week, every time he had to vacate Ron's living room, he went straight up the Serpentine and sat with the parakeets in their little clearing. Ephra was secretly fairly certain it meant he was going a bit mad, but if he didn't tell Ron about it, then it was between him and the birds, who weren't going to tell anyone. After all, he'd saved them from over-excited, free-roaming dogs on more than one occasion.

As he reached the edge of the water, the sharp November air bit down hard on the tip of his nose. Ephra cracked open Ron's flask and rested it against his top lip. He only intended to use the warmth to stave off further assaults, but the earthy aroma floated through him and he took his first sip without thinking. A deep sigh erupted from his chest and he felt some of the tension begin to slide out of his body. "Damn, that's good coffee."

A blackbird twittered at him and he smiled.

"I'd offer you some, but I don't think it would do you any good," Ephra replied, and continued on along the path.

When he got to the clearing, the parakeets swarmed him immediately. He let them flutter around him for a while, feeling the breeze and tickle of their small wings, before politely asking them if he could sit down. They obliged, all but a few retreating to the trees so that he could make himself comfortable without injuring anyone.

He sat quietly for a bit, listening to the small green creatures chattering to each other and working his way through his coffee. Two birds decided to swoop down onto his knee and pester him for some attention. He tapped each on the beak and then laughed to himself. The first chased after his hand and nipped at his finger, but it didn't hurt. Ephra gave it a gentle stroke under its chin.

"I'm getting far too comfortable around you guys, I'm sorry," he said. "It's weird. People always say 'a little birdie told me', but you're actually excellent secret keepers. I feel like I could tell you all anything. And you've not shat on me, not once."

The parakeets chirped at him happily and Ephra smiled. The one that had bitten him flew off and was quickly replaced by another. Ephra greeted it with a gentle fuss and a coo. "And why is it that you like me so much, hey?" He lowered his voice. "It's not really because you understand me, is it?"

The new bird hopped onto his finger and said, "Chak, chak, chak."

"Mmm," Ephra replied. "No, I didn't think so either. It's a nice thought, though."

In response, the bird flew up onto his head and began pulling at his hair. "Hey, hey! I'm not a seed ball! That hurts." Ephra flapped his hands around his head until it stopped. "Thank you, good grief."

He let out a deep sigh and took a sip from the flask. He'd almost emptied it already. The hot liquid made him feel warm and comfortable. *Is it possible to feel horrendous and wonderful at the same time?* he pondered, while the parakeets sang him a song.

He pulled a blade of grass from the ground and began to twist it around his finger. "I really don't want things to end with Ron, you know?"

There was a cheep from the top of his head.

"I know, I know that's what Halwyn's after. I can feel it in my gut. That's what he meant when he said my work was enthusiastic, but not good." Ephra scoffed. He felt little feet bounce with aggression against his scalp. "I don't want to write these books any more. It's endless, and I hate it and I just want to stop."

The bird on his knee chirped in.

"Well, yes, I know I'm contracted and I have to finish this one."

"Tweet."

"I don't have to stop seeing Ron, though, do I? Halwyn can't make me do that."

There was a sudden chorus from the trees that Ephra took to mean, "No."

"No, *no.* It's got nothing to do with Halwyn, quite right. I can see and be with and love whoever I want." Ephra knocked back the dregs from the flask. "And I love Ron," he said. "I love Ron!"

He threw his arms up in the air and the birds spiralled around him. He laughed, only then realising that maybe Ron had made his coffee a touch 'Irish'. His thoughts were starting to grow fuzzy around the edges, and the whirl of coloured birds seemed to knot itself into a twister of bright green ribbon. It span so fast he felt as though his body was being sucked up off the ground.

Ephra blinked heavily. "I should lie down."

He was cold, cold to the bone, but the space around him felt airless. There was no wind, no chill, just a complete lack of warmth. Only his hands and feet felt anything close to heat, because it was hard to tell the difference between heat and the burning pain of friction.

He was pushing. He didn't know what he was pushing, because wherever he was, it was pitch black.

But the thing was hard and heavy and took all the strength in his body to move, he knew that much.

A metallic smell filled his nostrils; the smell of his own blood. He could feel the wet slick of it on his soles and palms, where the grit of the floor and whatever was in front of him had grated away his skin. The viscous fluid made it hard to grip. He took every small step and push with care, but it wasn't enough.

He slipped, and the great hard mass bore down on him immediately, scraping him across the floor. He felt his body crunch and pop, but the mass continued to drive him down relentlessly, pushing him back the way they'd come. He could barely breathe, but he stayed conscious long enough to see and hear the crack of lightning that split his world apart.

At 4PM, Ephra awoke to a parakeet pecking him on the nose.

He grunted and flailed around, disorientated and unable to form a solid thought. The bird flapped in his face and hopped off. His hand followed it, maybe to apologise. He narrowly missed the parakeet and smacked the ground instead. Ephra hissed and dug his fingers into the dirt.

He lay with his eyes closed for a couple of minutes, trying to stop the world from spinning, trying to summon any kind of language. Eventually he managed, "Sorry."

He felt the little critter press against the back of his hand and opened his eyes. The bird was eyeing him with an expression of deep concern, if that was possible. Ephra recognised the look and tried to find some concern for himself, but his emotions seemed to be very far away. He felt numb where he should be scared and he knew that was wrong.

The parakeet clamped its beak around the edge of Ephra's pointer finger and tugged. Ephra nodded slowly. "Up."

It hopped backwards and Ephra flattened his hand into the ground and pushed himself upright. His head swam; he felt like it might fly off if he didn't stay perfectly still for a minute or two. "*Fuck me.*"

Two words, that was good. Ephra smiled, but he couldn't say that he was happy. The bird next to him still looked worried.

"Feet," Ephra said, and the parakeet nodded.

He sat still for a moment, trying to recall the order of movements that lead to one finding their feet. When he couldn't, he decided to go with the flow and see what happened. Somewhere in the tangle of limbs that followed, Ephra managed to summon one full coherent thought: "That wasn't alcohol."

No, Ephra had been drunk many times, and it had never left him in this state before. Something was very wrong. With that realisation, the fear hit. "I need Ron."

A second parakeet flew down from the trees and the two birds seemed to have a brief exchange before parakeet number two flew off again. Ephra heard it flutter through the treeline and hoped he was going to get help. He snorted at himself.

The remaining bird chakked at him with determination. Ephra nodded. "Okay."

He pushed his palm into the ground and rolled onto his knees.

"Chirp."

"Hang on," Ephra said, because his body parts were trying to float and the grass beneath him seemed to be crawling. He took a deep breath and pulled one foot up underneath his body.

"Chak chak."

"Right." Ephra sunk all of his weight into the ball of his foot and shoved at the ground below him. He practically rocketed to his feet, then lost his balance immediately and ran straight for the nearest tree. A flurry of green birds shot out of the branches as he knocked into the trunk.

He clung to the tree for as long as he needed, then pushed away slowly. As his eyes passed over his hands it looked, for a moment, as if they were covered in blood, but they couldn't be. There was no blood on the tree. He touched it to make sure. "No, no blood."

He tottered back into the clearing, all of his weight on his toes, like gravity couldn't get a hold of his heels. The parakeet who'd been helping him through everything was sitting on the flask. It chirped at him.

"Bend?"

"Chak."

Ephra sighed. He bent and picked up the flask, immediately regretting the decision. The grass beneath his feet turned into angry green waves. Ephra blinked rapidly, trying his best not to vomit, and straightened up, flask in hand.

"One foot," he said, meaning one step at a time.

His feathery assistant chirped again and flew up onto his head.

"Coming?" Ephra asked.

It tweeted and stayed put.

"Okay." Ephra turned very carefully, trying to stand tall to stop his new companion from falling off, and began the trudge back to Knightsbridge in the dimming daylight.

It was slow at first. Ephra's balance was all over the place and he relied on the park fences a lot. He navigated purely by instinct and the occasional chak. When he got to the bridge, he walked up the slope and left the park to walk along the main street and use the park wall as his crutch. He could feel himself growing more stable; as he walked, his weight seemed to shift back towards his heels. But he dared not look at his hands. Every time he did, he got brief flashes of blood, like he couldn't quite shake what he'd experienced while he was unconscious. It couldn't be real, though. There was nothing on the wall and nothing on Ron's flask.

There is nothing on Ron's flask. There is nothing on Ron's flask.

He repeated the thought over and over, partly because he needed reminding, partly because it was comforting to have a whole thought again.

Every now and then, Ephra needed to stop to catch his breath. The street lights were on by the time he'd found his way out of the park, and their amber light made his ears ring. Whenever he started to panic, the parakeet on his head made quiet cooing noises to distract him. He would raise his hand and let the little bird nuzzle it, afraid to pet it properly in case he hurt it with his terrible motor function. When his breathing evened out, the bird would chirp and Ephra would start his march again.

Finally, he reached Ron's house and stumbled up the steps. He went to knock, but Ron already had the door open. "Ephra, what's wrong? Are you okay?"

"What was in the coffee?" Ephra slurred. "I, I

thought it was alcohol, but now …" He glanced at his own hands and winced at the sight of them. "Something's wrong."

Ron looked at him in confusion, then a light flickered on. His face went pale. "I used the wrong milk."

Ephra peered up at him. "Wrong milk?"

Ron looked as if he might cry. He put his hand over his mouth and nose and let the air in his lungs escape through one whistly nostril. Then he said, very slowly, like he was talking to a child, "It's nothing, just a herbal thing. It'll wear off, but you should come in and sit down. I'll make you a nice normal cup of coffee." He began to guide Ephra inside, taking the flask from his hands.

"Wait …" Ephra said, mainly because he felt a bit sick, but also because there was a thought bubbling to the surface. "Did you drug me?"

Ron squeezed his eyes shut. "I'm so sorry, Ephra. I promise, I really, *really* didn't mean to. It's a herbal remedy that I offer to clients in very small doses to help them sleep, but I must have grabbed the wrong jug and used it like regular milk in your flask."

"Oh," Ephra said, "That was silly." It was the closest thing to a good scolding he could manage. Now that he had an explanation, now that he had Ron's warm arm wrapped around him, he found that he was too sleepy and dizzy to mind that his boyfriend had drugged him. When he looked at his hands all the blood was gone; the fear and panic were slipping away.

Is he my boyfriend? Ephra managed to think. *I am living in his house.*

Ron hefted him onto the sofa and helped him out of his coat and shoes. He wrapped Ephra tightly in a blanket, and told him not to move while he got him something to drink. It was only after Ron had left the room that Ephra remembered the bird on his head and went to pet it. But it was gone. He frowned, but then there came a tap at the window. Two parakeets sat outside watching him. He waved at them like a toddler, his fingers curling in on themselves. They chirped loud enough for him to hear through the glass, then fluttered off.

Ephra sat with a grin on his face. They were very good birds. He scooched down on the sofa and rested his cheek against the top of the cushions. His eyes fell on Sticks, who was peering at him from her tank.

Suddenly all his words came flying back. "Sticks!" he said. "Sticks! Jus' the woman I wanted to see." He lurched over to the tank with a burst of energy and leant right over, petting her smooth grey head. She tickled his wrist with her tongue. "Do you want to come out, hey? I don't mind, you can climb up if you want. Sorry, I don't really know how to pick you up."

As if she understood, Sticks did a little jump and

looped her long body over his neck. Ephra stood up carefully. "You're a clever girlie, Sticks. That was great!" He wandered back to the sofa, and Sticks slithered into his lap, resting her head on his hand. "Why didn't you want to do this before, hey?" Ephra scratched her chin. "It's much more comfortable for both of us."

She tickled him again, eliciting a drunken chuckle. "I swear to you, Sticks, you're the best snake."

Sticks looked up at him, beady eyes – like two silver ball-bearings – fixed on his face.

"Sometimes, I feel like I know you from another life or something. It's weird. I guess that's why I was scared. You remind me of something bad."

Sticks pressed her snout into his hand reassuringly.

"And Ron, Ron feels like something I've been waiting for, for an eternity," Ephra said, breathlessly. He wasn't quite sure he knew where the words were coming from. He wasn't thinking before he said them, but he knew they were his by how easily they came. He felt giddy, almost manic. "I'm not going to let this go, Sticks. I know it's early, but I can't. I promise, I swear it. I love Ron."

There was a small clatter behind him as Ron re-entered the room, a mug in each hand. Ephra turned to look at him. His mouth was a little agape. "You two look comfortable," he managed.

"We are." Ephra grinned. "We're best friends

now."

Ron shuffled around the sofa awkwardly and set the drinks down on the table. "Shall I put her back, so you don't spill anything on her?"

Ephra looked down at Sticks' face. She seemed to nod. "That seems wise," Ephra responded.

Ron picked up Sticks and carried her back to safety.

"Did you hear what I said to Sticks?" Ephra asked.

Ron smiled. "I might have."

"Oh," Ephra picked up his coffee and took a mouthful. It looked darker than normal and felt gritty on his tongue. "What's in this?"

"Just some charcoal to help pull the henbane out of your system."

"Oh, okay." Ephra took another mouthful and swallowed. "I meant it, though, what I said. I love you. I don't really understand how I could have fallen this fast, but I have." Ephra swished his thumb back and forth along the edge of his mug in time with his words. Ron was stirring his tea, face shrouded in his hair. "The moment I saw you I started swearing in my head because I just knew. Honestly, I'm surprised I've managed to keep it in for so long." The more he said the more stupid he felt, and Ron still didn't look up. "Sorry, I don't want to put you on the spot. I know it's insane. I've gone from not being able to speak to not being able to stop talking, so please shut me up."

Ron finally turned and put a hand on Ephra's leg. He hesitated, then gave it an odd little squeeze. "You should get some sleep, Ephra. Okay?" Ephra put his coffee down before he could drop it. His hands were suddenly shaking with the fear that he'd fucked up. Ron took them in his. "I'll be right here, though, to make sure you're okay. I really am so sorry this happened, Ephra."

Ephra pulled his hands away and dragged the blanket up around his ears. He slumped sideward onto the sofa. He didn't want to be there anymore. He didn't want to be anywhere anymore.

Wouldn't it be nice to stop existing? he thought, and the words echoed around his head.

The next morning, Ephra found himself alone on the sofa, swaddled in blankets, feeling like absolute shite. Ron was sat on the seat opposite, reading a crime novel with blood splattered across the cover. He looked up as Ephra began to wriggle in an attempt to gain his freedom.

"Morning, sleepyhead. How are you feeling?"

"Ugh," Ephra responded. It was all he could manage.

Ron frowned. "Are you hungry? Thirsty?"

"Both," Ephra said, finally freeing his arms. As he sat up, fragments of the day before came back to him: the bird in his hair, no weight in his heels, blood on his hands. "Did you drug me yesterday, or did I dream that?"

Ron grimaced. "I – I did. I'm so sorry, Ephra. It really was an accident."

Ephra rubbed his throbbing temples. "Mmm, feels like a car accident. What was it that you dosed me with?"

"H-Henbane milk," Ron stuttered. "I put the jug on the wrong shelf and …"

When Ephra looked up, Ron was staring intently at a spot on the floor. He could see the tears brimming along Ron's bottom lashes.

Ephra took a moment to let it all sink in. Ron had drugged him. Accidentally, yes, but it had still happened.

Am I okay with that? he thought. *Am I okay that I was so out of control?*

Anything could have happened to him. Ephra had passed out in the middle of Kensington Gardens, completely alone, except for the parakeets. And then he'd staggered through London, hallucinating and then … and then…

I told him I love him, Ephra realised. He felt all the blood drain from his face. *I sodding told him that I meant it.*

Ephra and Ron's eyes met for a fluttering second. "I … I have to go back to the flat today," Ephra said quickly.

"Oh … okay. Do you want me to call you a taxi?"

Ephra shook his head. "No, I imagine the walk will do me some good."

"Right, of course. Have a glass of water first, though, and something to eat."

"I'd rather not."

"Please?" Ron pressed. When Ephra glanced at him the pained expression on his face was intolerable.

"I'm – I'm not mad, Ron," Ephra said firmly.

"You're not?"

Ephra sighed. "Okay, maybe I am a bit, but … I just need to go home, Ron. I need to be alone for a second."

Ron chewed at his bottom lip fretfully, then he got up and went to the kitchen. Ephra heard the cupboards bang, the water run. Ron returned with a bottle of water and a breakfast bar. "Here, for the journey. And you should really take my sunglasses, too. You'll probably be light sensitive for a while."

"Okay."

Ron had been right about the sunglasses. Despite the overcast sky, daylight without them would have been unbearable on the walk home. Even the strip light in the hallway outside Ephra's flat was too much.

The moment he got inside, Ephra shut the door and examined his flat in total darkness. It was a relief, not only for his eyes, but for his heart. The comforting sense of being alone nestled in around his shoulders.

Home sweet home. He huffed. *Never thought I'd think that about this place.*

He took off Ron's glasses tentatively, making sure he could deal with the flat's murky, north-facing light without them. Happy his eyes could adjust, he slipped the sunnies into his coat pocket and hooked the coat over the door handle.

Ephra's stomach growled. The breakfast bar Ron had given him had lasted about two bites, and suddenly he realised that he hadn't eaten properly since breakfast the morning before. He'd promised Ron that he'd get something while he was out in the park, but had then drunk himself into a drugged-up stupor and slept straight through dinner time.

Maybe I should have let Ron make me something, Ephra thought.

He plodded into the kitchen and opened his fridge. It was empty, except for an expired bottle of milk and a lump of cheese that had grown new friends.

Ephra sighed. *Of course, if I'd let him make me something that would have given him more time to bring up the 'I love you'.*

He shut the fridge and turned. Halwyn's massive gift basket sat smugly on the kitchen table.

"Fuck, I'm going to have to eat you, aren't I?" The pink cellophane glinted mischievously as he moved towards it. "Your muffins better not be mouldy."

Ephra undid the purple bow and peeled back the packaging. The muffins had, thankfully, not gone mouldy, but they were stale and tasted a little bit like plastic. He sat and ate and listened to the clock tick.

"I think I might prefer grey, dull and painless to embarrassment and heartbreak," he said aloud to no-one and nothing in particular. "Maybe Halwyn's right?"

The words made him gag a little, but he wasn't completely unconvinced by them. Maybe Ephra's relationship with Ron would make him a worse writer. Maybe it would ruin his career for good. After all, how much emotional torture could one person go through before everything they were broke down and became something entirely different?

Like a writer who can't stand the sight of words.

Ephra finished off another muffin and then plodded into his bedroom. He stripped down to his boxers and slid under the duvet. The sheets smelt musty and a little of BO.

He didn't say it back, he thought as he closed his eyes. His heart dropped. His guts, his chest, his back, his head, his soul: everything ached.

I'm better off alone. I've always been better off alone.

He whistled through the air so fast that he thought the wind might blind him, or the sound might deafen him. He pushed his hands flat against his ears and squeezed his elbows together in front of his eyes, trying to guard them.

In the brief moments he was able to keep his eyes open, he caught sight of the land below. It surprised him. It wasn't what he had expected to see. There was a swirling river with sandy shores and well irrigated farmland to either side.

I'm not dead, *he thought,* but I will be.

He couldn't tell if he was crying with fear, or if it was just the sharp wind cutting at his eyes that caused the stream of tears to skirt along his cheeks and up the sides of his hands. There was nothing he could do. Soon he would be dead, and once he was …

The land below loomed ever closer. It was all he could do not to openly sob. Then he felt something hot and burning clutch his leg. His hip made an almighty pop that shuddered through him. The noise that erupted from his mouth lost itself in the wind.

His descent slowed, but continued, until finally the silvery waters enveloped his head. Only his head. He gasped and spluttered for air as whatever had hold of his ankle dunked him in and out of the river. Above the raging waters, he thought he heard laughter; seething, malicious laughter.

Then his ears began to ring, his vision began to tunnel.

I deserve this, *he thought,* I deserve everything I get.

Ephra sat up in bed so fast that he cracked his head on the top bar of the headboard and sent a bolt of pain skittering around his skull. He let out a wet sob and rubbed his crown weakly. He was still gasping, unable to catch his breath; his whole body was drenched in cold sweat.

Downstairs, the shop alarm was going off. It was a high-pitched whine that grated against his eardrums. Ephra clamped his hands over his ears and knotted the tips of his fingers into his hair.

"What the fuck?" Ephra shuddered. *"What the actual fuck?"*

He brought his knees up and rested his forehead on

them for a moment. He tried to focus on the sound of his breath echoing against his palms, tried to get a hold of the pattern and make his lungs work with him, instead of against him.

It took a while, but his breathing finally returned to a steady in and out. *You're okay. You're okay,* he told himself. *This isn't the first time the alarm has gone off. You know what to do.*

He nodded, alone in the dark, and slowly removed his hands from his ears. The alarm went off every time there was a power cut, so he tested his bedside lamp first. When it didn't turn on, he felt for the drawer underneath and yanked it open. He scrabbled around inside until his hand found the thick plastic headband of his headphones and wriggled them free, pulling the cups over his ears quickly.

Even without anything playing through them, the noise cancelling improved the situation considerably. Ephra breathed in as deeply and slowly as he could, then growled as he let it all out again.

Why is this my life? He pulled the duvet off himself and shivered. *This feels like a dressing gown day … or night, as the case may be.*

He lifted himself up onto his feet and scuffed his way to the bathroom. The cold tiles felt like ice, but Ephra's slippers were all the way in the living room and he wasn't about to make that journey in his current state.

He ran the tap and splashed his face with lukewarm water, trying to get rid of some of the stickiness of his nightmare, without brewing an icicle on his nose.

Ephra wiped his wet hands over his skin and patted the rest of himself down with a hand towel from the laundry basket. There was no way he was leaving the flat on a day like this, so he didn't need to be clean, just dry and comfortable. Clean could wait for better days.

He wandered over to the back of the bathroom door and grabbed his dressing gown, bundled himself up and listened. The alarm was still going off. If he tried to go back to sleep now, he would be awake again the moment his headphones got knocked off his head.

Not to mention I'm apparently incapable of getting a good night's sleep anyway. Except at Ron's. Ephra pinched the bridge of his nose and rubbed his sinuses. *Let's not think about that right now.*

There was only one thing for it, really: crack open the laptop and get to work.

Ephra made himself a coffee and settled down in his armchair. It hadn't been that long, but it felt weird to be back in his living room with the white glow of his laptop burning his retinas. He blinked rapidly to adjust to the light, typed in his password and checked the battery life and time. It was 5AM, but the machine had a good three hours of life left in it. He could probably do something with that, and then maybe try a nap if the alarm had stopped.

He cracked open his work-in-progress and started to take apart the first page, erasing all the details that made the characters *unsuitable*, as Halwyn had suggested. Every deletion and correction made Ephra's heart hurt a little. He thought the love interest was wonderful, so full of joy and warmth. All he wanted was to show how someone like his protagonist could connect with someone like that.

How someone like me could connect with someone like Ron. Ephra sighed. *But did we really connect? I clearly felt something he didn't.* And *he drugged me.*

The tearful expression on Ron's face as he'd explained what had happened flashed through Ephra's mind.

"He was genuinely upset about it, though," he told himself.

He really had been. After all, if Ephra had learnt anything about Ron in the past few weeks, it was that Ron was *terrible* at keeping his emotions hidden. Every flicker of happiness or pain Ron felt wriggled to the surface.

"And he took care of me ..."

Yes, there was that, too. Ron hadn't just felt bad about drugging Ephra, he'd looked after him. He hadn't taken advantage, even when it probably would have been pretty easy to convince Ephra to do anything. And when Ephra had made him uncomfortable by blurting out his feelings, Ron hadn't sent him packing. In fact, Ephra vaguely remembered that, after he'd slumped over like a grumpy blanket burrito, Ron had scooped his feet up onto the sofa and gently caressed the top of his head. And he must have sat there reading all night to make sure he was okay.

"Oh, for fuck's sake!" Ephra slapped his palm against his forehead. "I'm the one shitting this up this time, aren't I?"

By 8AM Ephra was showered, dressed and out of his flat. He had collected up the mess of pink packaging and stale food left on his kitchen table, marched it down the stairs, and lobbed it straight into the building's shared skip as he came out of the back entrance.

"There," he said, thumping the lid down. "That's what I should have done in the first place."

He made a sharp, determined turn and began the walk to Ron's. He wanted to get there early, just in case Ron had taken a morning client. Ron's place had been so tidy after the first day they'd met that Ron had been talking about expanding his availability. If he thought

Ephra was out of the picture, he might have gone ahead and started booking people in.

Would he do that, though? Assume you weren't coming back? Ephra pondered as he strode across the park. *He did drug you. And you did spend a good chunk of the last twenty-four hours thinking about how you might be better off alone.*

He shook his head. Even if Ron had booked a client, what would it matter? He'd be there before nine, and if the client had already arrived, he'd hang around outside. It was Ron: joyful, loving, caring Ron. He was worth waiting around for.

What if he doesn't want to see me? Ephra bit his tongue.

He looked up from the pavement and stopped dead in his tracks, realising he'd walked past Ron's house while buried deep in thought. He blinked, a little alarmed that he couldn't really remember the traipse through the park. Then he sighed and, in typical British fashion, he took his phone out and pretended to check it before walking back the way he'd come. This day was likely to be embarrassing enough without anyone watching him do an awkward about-turn.

Ephra tucked his phone back into his pocket as he jogged up the steps to Ron's door. Before he could let himself hesitate, he rang the doorbell and gave a sharp knock for good measure. There was silence from inside.

Ephra peered through the frosted glass. The ground floor appeared to be dark, and there was no sign of movement.

He rang the doorbell again. Still no movement, but there was a loud groan from somewhere within.

Concerned, Ephra crouched down and lifted the letterbox. "Ron, it's Ephra. Are you okay?"

There was a bang and clatter and a, "*Sugar!*" Then came a pause, then a shuffle of feet. When Ron finally answered the door Ephra did a double take. Ron's bouncy 'joyboat' demeanour was completely absent. He looked pale, his curls were completely crushed in some places and sticking up in others, and he had visible dark circles under his eyes. Not to mention, he was wearing yesterday's clothes and a king-sized duvet.

"Ephra," he said quietly, clearly embarrassed. "I – I wasn't expecting you."

It took every ounce of willpower in Ephra's body not to press his hand to Ron's face and stroke his thumb along his cheek.

"I'm sorry," he said instead. "I probably should have phoned, but I was in action mode rather than thinking mode." Ephra cracked a little smile, trying to set Ron at ease. "Are you okay?"

"Yes," Ron said. "Do you want to come in?"

"If that's okay with you?"

Ron nodded and took a step back. "Of course. You'll have to excuse the mess, though."

"I'm sure it's not –" Ephra stopped mid-sentence as he took a step around the great wall of duvet and saw the state of the hallway. There were stacks of books and scattered pages littered all over the floor, and what appeared to be an entire basket of perfectly clean laundry cascading down the stairs.

Ephra looked at Ron. Ron looked at the floor and said, "When you didn't phone yesterday, I thought …"

Ephra threw his arms around Ron, duvet and all. He squeezed as tightly as he could for as long as he could. The front door slammed closed with a gust of wind and they both flinched, but Ephra hung on a little longer. When he let go, Ron seemed to have some of the colour back in his cheeks.

"Let's sit down and talk, alright?"

Ron nodded and allowed Ephra to tow him into the living room. Sticks eyed Ephra as they entered. He gave her a little wave and she slithered behind one of her logs, as if to give them some privacy. Ephra and Ron perched on the sofa, Ron still engulfed in his abundance of bedding. The white cover made Ron look rather marshmallow-like and Ephra couldn't help but smile at him as he began.

"I just want to explain why I left, and why I'm here, okay?"

Ron nodded again.

Ephra took a deep breath. "Remember how I said I

don't like not being in control?"

"Yes," Ron said, his voice dry.

"Well, what happened, that was the most out of control I've ever been. It felt … it felt like my body was drifting apart, like I didn't have command of anything. I was seeing things and –"

"Ephra, I –" Ron started.

"No, listen. I know how sorry you are. And I know you didn't mean to. You looked after me, even when I made you uncomfortable, even when it would have been very easy to take advantage –"

"I would never!" Ron yelped in horror.

Ephra put his hand on Ron's knee. "I know, and that's why I'm here. Don't get me wrong, I'm still a little shaken, and you are absolutely never to do that to me again, but I was really rather hoping that we could pretend the whole thing never happened, and continue to see how things go?"

Ron's eyes widened in surprise. "Are you sure?"

"Yes. I like you, and while drugging me is about as bad as mistakes can get, I know that's what it was – a mistake." Ephra smiled. "I don't want to end this at the first hurdle, do you?"

"No!" Ron took Ephra's hand from his knee and squeezed it between his palms. "I would very much like to forget the *whole thing* too."

Ephra ignored the little pang in his chest at the

emphasis Ron put on the phrase, 'whole thing'. He decided to firmly push the 'I love you' elephant in the room right up into the corner, where Sticks could eat it if she felt up to the challenge.

"Right." Ephra laughed. "Great, well." He looked around the room. "Do you think maybe you could use some fresh air?"

Ron winced. "Yeah … a walk might be a good idea. I'll clean this all up this evening."

"I do rather like the mess if I'm honest. It's kind of a nice aesthetic. Homely." Ephra ran his thumb over Ron's.

"Still, as Sticks loves to point out, it's not exactly a practical lifestyle choice when you're as clumsy as I am." Ron chuckled. "I should go take a shower and change."

Ephra pointed to a stack of books. "I can make a start on those while you're gone, if you like? That case there, right?"

Ron blushed and nodded. "You really don't have to."

"If I don't, Sticks will just glower at me from her tank the entire time you're up there."

Ron laughed, "Okay then," and set off up the stairs.

About an hour later, Ron re-appeared with freshly cast curls, a set of clean clothes and a gorgeous smile and asked, "How do you feel about boats?"

The next thing he knew, Ephra was staring at a string of rowboats in Hyde Park, wondering when was a good time to tell Ron he couldn't swim. As it happened, the moment passed as Ron dashed off to pay for the rental. He returned with two oars and a spectacular flutter of golden hair, before Ephra's thoughts could catch up with his tongue.

"You okay?" Ron asked.

"Yeah, I've just, uh, never been in one of these before."

Ron nodded. "Not to worry. I'm something of an expert when it comes to boats. I'll hold it steady while you get in and sit down." Ron jumped confidently into the centre of the boat and took his seat, then grabbed onto the dock. "Get as low as you can and aim to put your feet in the middle. It'll reduce the amount of rocking. Oh, and sit down as soon as you can. You'll feel sturdier once you're seated."

Ephra looked at him doubtfully. *Tell him you can't bloody swim*, he thought.

"I promise, if you fall in, I'll fish you out." Ron winked like he could hear what Ephra was thinking.

Ephra sighed at himself, then crouched and stretched one leg down off the dock. Even with his leg fully extended it felt like the boat was miles away, but he managed to plant his foot fairly square in the centre. The other followed shortly after and he landed on the seat with a thump that made the boat wobble.

Ron laughed. "Very graceful for a beginner."

Ephra resisted the urge to poke his tongue out like a child. "I'm sure if you'd woken at 5AM to the shop alarm downstairs blaring, you'd stick the dismount just as well."

Ron grimaced. "Tell me that's not really how you woke up?"

Ephra smiled and shrugged. "I probably would have been up anyway. I don't sleep particularly well in general."

"You said you slept well at mine?"

"Oh, I did!" Ephra laughed awkwardly. "I slept like a log at your place, but I can't seem to take so much as a cat nap at mine without waking up drenched in sweat." The expression on Ron's face was leaning way too far in the direction of horror, so Ephra added, "It's a figure of speech."

"It's really not."

"Hyperbole, then." Ephra winked. "Come on, let's

get this boat on the road."

Ron chuckled, untied the boat's tether and set the oars in place. Ephra got the sense they were both too knackered to debate his sleep crisis any further. His head was foggy, and the bags under Ron's eyes were still pretty puffy. However, Ephra didn't need his full faculties to know that boating was something Ron enjoyed and was eager to share. Despite his visible lack of sleep, Ron was beaming, and they hadn't even got going yet.

Ron pushed the boat away from the dock and began to steer them confidently out into the middle of the Serpentine. As he pulled at the oars, Ephra noted that this seemed to be exactly what the lean musculature of Ron's frame was built for. He marvelled at how seamlessly Ron moved them through the water, not a hint of effort on his face nor strain in his body. Ron was, in fact, so completely relaxed that he looked more comfortable rowing the boat than he did lying on his own sofa.

"This is where you love to be, isn't it?" Ephra said.

Ron nodded. "I would sit out here every day if I could. It's beautiful."

Ephra gazed at the water and watched the light dance and glitter across its surface. "It is that," he agreed. He thought about what he had imagined being on the water would feel like and closed his eyes.

The wind nibbled at his skin and played with his

hair. It felt a little like he was flying, except there was a constant surge of motion beneath his feet as Ron sped them along. He held onto that feeling, analysing it, memorising the vibration. It was moving forward. It was Ron and him together in the perfect place.

"I meant to tell you, I can't swim," Ephra said, eyes still closed.

Ron slowed his pace, pulling them to a steady halt. "You can't?"

"No, I never had reason to learn, so no-one ever bothered to teach me." Ephra blinked a few times to clear his eyes. As they refocused, he took in Ron's concerned expression again and grinned. "Oh, no, don't worry! I'm fine!"

"You sure?"

Ephra put a hand over Ron's. "Yes, absolutely." He leant back, and Ron began to paddle again, slightly slower. "It was just, I was thinking about how I never would have done this if I hadn't met you, that's all. But moments before I met you, I was stood, probably right there, wishing I knew what it felt like to be out on the water." Ephra pointed to the bank.

"It does seem like the Fates might have intervened on our behalf, doesn't it?"

Ephra chuckled. "Between this, my books on your shelf, and the bloody bird that led me to you, I'd say so, yeah."

"A bird led you to me?"

Ephra stared down into the water, tempted to touch it, but then his hand would get frozen. "I was sort of heading in that direction anyway," he said. "But I'd been talking to this song thrush, and then it flew off and, next thing I knew, I was stopping you from falling into the river."

"Huh," Ron responded. "That's interesting. And what did you say to this thrush exactly?"

Ephra felt a burning in his cheeks that wasn't the wind. "I might have been having a rant about being a romance writer who'd never been in love."

Ron's feet lifted from the bottom of the boat as he let out a belly laugh. "And you think the birds don't really understand you?"

Ephra rolled his eyes. "They're birds, Ron."

Ron nodded. "Mmm ... and they really have a soft spot for you."

Ephra was about to protest when a fully grown mallard landed in his lap and let out a happy quack. He sat, open-mouthed, staring at the green-headed male as Ron roared with laughter.

"This shit is getting weird," Ephra said to the duck. "I mean, what is it about me exactly? Did I use too much product this morning? Does my hair look like a rather large moorhen?"

The duck quacked again.

"That's very useful, thank you." Ephra huffed. "Bloody birds." He peered over at Ron, who was still trying to recover, then looked sheepishly down at the mallard and whispered, "Sorry, I didn't really mean that." The mallard flapped his wings, sending a flurry of water droplets hurtling at Ephra. Ephra shielded his face a moment too late.

"Right, well, I said I was sorry and now I'm soaking. Are we even?" he asked when the duck had finished showering him.

The duck snapped its bill at Ephra and flew off. Ephra watched him soar, then skid to a graceful stop on the water near the bank. There was a woman with some young children throwing food out into the Serpentine.

Ephra turned back to Ron. Ron was looking at him so intently, and with such a perfect smile on his face that Ephra had to look away again immediately. "W-what?" he stuttered, peering sideward.

Ron's lips twisted with discomfort. He pulled the oars in a bit and let them sit in the boat. Then he tucked his hair behind his ears and said, "There's something I really want to say to you, but I'm a little uncertain as to how you're going to react."

"Okay?" Ephra said, his stomach bubbling with nerves. "Do I ask why you're uncertain, or what it is you want to tell me?"

Ron grazed his canine back and forth across his lip;

it didn't help Ephra feel any less tense. "See, I'm uncertain because you said you wanted to pretend like what happened two nights ago didn't happen, and I'm worried that saying what I want to say will, maybe … I don't know, force a conversation you're not ready to have yet?"

"What d'you mean?"

"Well, you seemed very ready to have this particular conversation the other night, while you were drugged up to your eyeballs, but I –" Ephra suddenly caught on and his faced contorted so sharply that Ron stopped mid-sentence. He paused for a moment, then said, "Ah, never mind then."

Ephra scanned Ron's face. He was still smiling serenely, but his eyes looked lifeless and grey. "I'm sorry, I shouldn't have pulled a face."

"No, no. I shouldn't have brought it up. You said –"

"I know what I said, Ron." Ephra scrunched his face up. "I just, I may have only said it because I was embarrassed and I thought I'd made you uncomfortable." He pointed his face at the sky, letting a groan of awkwardness rumble in his chest. "But if you wanted to add something to that conversation that you feel is important I hear, I'll listen."

"Oh," Ron said. "That's good, because I did really want to say that I love you, too. It just didn't seem right when you weren't really yourself."

Ephra blinked at the sky for a moment, then gradually let his eyes drop back down to Ron. Ron's head was hunched into his shoulders a little.

This idiot's nervous that I won't say it again. This ridiculous fool thought I didn't mean it.

Ephra lurched across the boat and planted his mouth against Ron's. He kissed him deeply, then softly, then wrapped his arms around him and propped his head on his shoulder.

"I did mean it. I do love you, Ron."

Ron breathed a deep sigh of relief against Ephra's ear. "Thank *fuck* for that."

The moment Ephra sent Halwyn his rewritten chapters a sense of impending doom slipped over him. His mouth went dry, his heart started thundering, and by the time Ron found him lying on the living room floor, head under the coffee table, he was fairly certain he was having a panic attack.

"Nothing's going to happen, Ephra. The worst he can do is make you write it again."

"And again, and again, and again, and again," Ephra panted.

Ron sat on the floor with him and held his hand.

"And I'll stick with you. And if I need to, I'll buy you out of this stupid contract."

Ephra jolted upright, banging his head on the table. He hissed, then said, "You can't do that. I can't let you do that, that's insane."

Ron shrugged. "It's not like I don't have the money, and I hate seeing you like this."

"But –"

"The offer's there, Ephra. You don't have to take it, but I don't want you to feel trapped anymore." Ron kissed his cheek.

Ephra sat there speechless. He wanted to cry. He felt like a boulder had been lifted off his shoulders.

Then his laptop pinged.

Ephra sighed and pulled it off the table. "He's sent me a meeting request."

There was no e-mail, no, 'I want to talk about x, y and z.' It was just a calendar invite for 2PM that afternoon. Ephra grumbled to himself, then hit 'accept' before he could dither over it any longer.

Ron took the laptop from him, propped it on the sofa, and pulled Ephra against his chest. "If he treats you like sugar, you tell him to shove his Dip Dab up his After Eight and come right back here."

Ephra chuckled. "I'll have to wash your mouth out with soap if you're not careful." He laced his fingers into Ron's hair and began to play with his curls, nervously.

Ron nuzzled his head further into Ephra's hand. "I don't know what you mean. I was simply suggesting a bizarre and slightly disgusting mixture of sweets."

Ephra leant up and nipped Ron's bottom lip. "That would explain why you always taste sharp and sugary at the same time."

"I think that's just the pomegranate I ate for breakfast."

"Hmm, I don't know. Let me check again."

Halwyn's office had been redecorated. It was still very, *very* pink, but now the whole room was baby vomit coloured. It immediately set Ephra on edge.

As usual, he had let himself into the office. In all the years Ephra had worked with him, Halwyn Tân had never been on time. Ephra was fairly certain it was a tactic, because even when Ephra was late, Halwyn wandered in precisely ten minutes later.

Ephra sat down stiffly and watched the minutes tick by on Halwyn's brand new *aubergine* replica of Big Ben. The motion of the hands made his stomach clench, so he closed his eyes.

He thought about Ron, played back the last few weeks with him on a loop, pictured his big goofy grin and chuckled to himself.

"What was that?" Halwyn said, bursting in through the glass door.

"Nothing you need to worry about." Ephra sighed, braced himself, and opened his eyes to the lurid pink office once more. "I love what you've done with the place."

"Do you?" Halwyn grinned. "I wanted to freshen it up, you know? I think the new look is very on brand."

"Yes, definitely," Ephra said, eyeing Halwyn's flowery blush suit.

Halwyn shuffled through some papers on his desk and then sat down. He steepled his fingers and rested his chin on the tips of his nails. "So, I think we both know why I called this meeting."

"Let me guess, my work is terrible?"

Halwyn did his best to look sympathetic; it came off as more of a sneer. "Yes, Ephra, I'm afraid it's rather appalling. Even with the rework you've done. If we don't figure this out soon, you won't be able to deliver on time and then –"

"You'll take my advance back. Yeah, yeah, yeah," Ephra breathed. "Only here's the thing, Hal, I don't really buy that."

Halwyn sat back, a frown of confusion on his brow. "What don't you buy?"

"Well, the thing is, my last four books were utter

twaddle. My characters were stereotypes, my plot lines had been done a thousand times, and frankly, the chemistry on the page left something to be desired."

"That's your opinion."

Ephra shook his head. "No, that's the truth, and you know it. And the stuff I've been writing for you this time, it's pretty much the same. The only difference is that I don't hate that I'm writing it."

Halwyn pursed his lips. "Whether you want to see it or not, Ephra, your quality has significantly decreased. And I think we both know what the issue really is."

Ephra let out a laugh and Halwyn looked taken aback. "There it is. Say it. Go on, I dare you."

Something in Halwyn's eyes flickered. His jaw tightened. "You need to break it off with whoever you're seeing."

"Why? Because you say so?"

Halwyn stood up abruptly. "Yes! Because I say so."

"I'm not going to do that, Halwyn."

Halwyn's whole body began to shake. His face went so red that Ephra thought he was about to explode. "You can't say no."

"I can, and I am."

"You're under contract."

"I'm under contract to write you a book. One more book, and I will give you that book for you to publish or trash as you see fit. After that, I am done with you."

Halwyn went pale. "*How* are you saying that to me?"

"Why shouldn't I say that to you? You manipulate me, you insult me, and now you're trying to wreck the beginnings of something real. And I won't let you do it, Halwyn. I made a promise to him and his goddamn snake, and I am not about to break it for some shit of a publisher and a career I never wanted in the first place." Ephra stood up and made to leave.

"Hang on," Halwyn said, so quietly that it made Ephra stop. "You made a promise to a snake?"

Ephra frowned at him. "Don't be a dick, Halwyn. Yes, the guy I'm in love with has a snake, and I promised her that I wouldn't let this relationship go."

Halwyn licked his lips. "This wouldn't happen to be a long grey snake, would it? Goes by the name of Sticks?"

Ephra's eyes widened in horror. "You know her? Do you know Ron, too?!"

Halwyn put his hand over his face and screamed into his palm. "*Shit!* I should have guessed that's why he didn't just *go away* like all the others. That absolute carrot."

Ephra stood, frozen to the spot, as Halwyn dragged the violet trench coat from the back of his chair and shoved his arms into it. *Why does he know Ron*, he thought, *why in the ever-loving fuck does he know Ron?*

Halwyn grabbed a set of car keys and barrelled towards him. He caught hold of Ephra's cuff and span him out of the door. "Come on, I need to have words with your new boyfriend."

"Fuck," was all Ephra could manage in response.

Halwyn Tân practically threw Ephra into the back of his immense black Mercedes, then drove west across London to Knightsbridge, taking every opportunity to speed that London traffic allowed. Ephra was silent for the entire drive, praying that Halwyn didn't really know Ron, and trying not to think about what that might mean.

Did they date? No, no. That can't be it. Ron would have recognised the name Halwyn, surely?

The closer they got to Ron's house, the further Ephra sank into the backseat. When Halwyn pulled up to Ron's front door, it was all Ephra could do not to lean out of the car and vomit into the gutter. There was bile sitting in his throat.

I can't deal with this. I can't deal with this.

Halwyn got out and ripped Ephra from the car, immediately trying to force him up the steps. Ephra shook him off.

"I can walk," he said, too quietly.

Halwyn smiled menacingly. "Of course you can. So be a love, wobble up the stairs and ask your boyfriend if he's got time for a quick chat."

Ephra looked at him. "Why can't you do it?"

Halwyn's whole face seemed to shift: his eyes darkened, his cheeks grew sallow. "Keep questioning me. I dare you."

Ephra leant away. Fear trickled down his spine. Part of him wanted to remain defiant, put up a good front. The other part suddenly had a funny feeling that doing so might mean his end.

He jogged up the stairs and made to knock the door, but as his knuckles touched the wood the door swung inwards.

"Ron?" Ephra called. "Are you in?"

There was no response. Ephra slipped through the door and checked the living room. It was empty. Not even Sticks. *Ah.*

Ephra turned to find Halwyn had followed him in, and almost jumped out of his skin.

"Where is he?" Halwyn seethed.

"Uh, I'm not sure, but Sticks isn't in her tank so –"

Halwyn let out a roar of frustration and whipped out his phone. He tapped the screen rapidly, then pressed the device to his ear. While they waited for Ron to pick up, Halwyn did not take his eyes off Ephra's. Ephra wanted to look down, or up, or anywhere, but there was something about Halwyn's gaze.

If you stare into the abyss, Ephra thought, *the abyss stares back.*

"Ron!" Halwyn yelled, with none of his usual cheer. "Yes, it's me. You know me, Halwyn, Ephra's publisher." He paused. "Yes, Ron. Yes, that is what that means. Now, *where are you?*"

There was a moment of silence. Ephra could just about hear Ron's voice on the other end. It seemed higher than usual, stressed. Ephra's mind was already spinning when Halwyn grabbed his wrist and started dragging him back towards the door. "Stay where you are, we'll meet you."

As Halwyn hung up, Ephra finally decided enough was enough and he needed to know what the hell was going on. He yanked himself free and stopped. "I'm not going anywhere with you until you explain what's happening!"

Halwyn practically snarled at him. "I don't have time for this, Ephra. Move yourself!"

"No."

The publisher's nostrils flared. "Okay, let's put this in terms that you'll understand. Your new fella used to work for me, back in the good old days."

"Ron? He's not an author."

"No." Halwyn said thoughtfully. "He was a driver of sorts. He used to ferry things around for me."

"Like your courier now?"

Halwyn smiled. "Something like that, Ephra."

"So, what? You think he'll break up with me because his old boss tells him to?"

"Yes, that's exactly what I think. Now will you walk with me, or would you rather I carry you?"

"You're mad," Ephra said, backing away from Halwyn slowly. "You're actually mad."

Halwyn let out a cackle. "Oh, Ephra, I'm far worse than mad. I'm *furious*." He let out an audible breath through his nose. "Now get the *fuck* outside."

Ephra took a moment and decided it was probably safer to be in a public place than stay inside Ron's house with this insanity. He stumbled around Halwyn, trying to give him a wide berth, and hopped out of the door and down the steps. He considered running, but then he thought about Ron, waiting for them wherever he was, and he knew he couldn't let him face Halwyn alone.

They found Ron waiting for them on the bridge over the Serpentine. His hair was an absolute mess, and Ephra didn't think it was just the wind that had tousled it. He wanted to run at him, fling his arms around him, and forget Halwyn out of existence, but Halwyn stopped short – about four metres away – and put his arm in front of Ephra to prevent him from going any further.

Ron looked up at the sound of Ephra's feet scuffling to a halt; there were obvious tears in his eyes. "I'm so sorry, Ephra. I didn't know. I really didn't know."

"Didn't know what?" Ephra asked.

"That you're –"

"Stop right there!" Halwyn interjected. "You don't get to tell him. You just get to end this before I end it for you."

"I – I –" Ron stuttered.

"Ron?" Ephra said, trying to wrap his head around Ron's hesitation. He'd thought Halwyn was crazy, but no; this was real insanity. "You can't seriously be – you promised, Ron, and I know you meant it."

Ron opened his mouth. Halwyn wagged his finger. "Just get it over with, Ron, dear."

Ron put his hands in his hair and started pacing. Ephra watched his feet stamp back and forth across the pavement. A high-pitched whistle began ringing in his ears. He couldn't understand what was going on; he couldn't believe Ron might actually end things because Halwyn *bloody* Tân told him to. The whistle grew so loud Ephra thought he might scream.

Then something behind Ron's feet shifted and Ephra blinked. He regained focus on reality just in time to see the smooth, grey body of a snake drop off the bridge and into the water. He rushed over to the side.

"Sticks!" he cried, but there was a sudden crack of lightning and Ephra's voice was lost in the thunder.

Ephra looked up at the cloudless sky in astonishment, then he noticed the chilling silence. The cars on the bridge had ground to a halt. A jogger on the footpath had frozen. And the river …

"What the hell is that?!" Ephra exclaimed.

Below them, the waters of the Serpentine had turned almost completely silver with fog, but through the cracks leapt ghostly forms: hands, feet, faces.

Halwyn leant on the stonework next to him. "You're asking after the wrong eternal tomb, Ephra. That there is the River Styx."

Ephra looked up at him in confusion, then stumbled backwards. Halwyn's face was no longer human. Sure, he had all of the component parts, but his eyes were ringed with blackened burns and his irises danced with actual flame.

"In case you're wondering, yes, that does make me Hades." Halwyn grinned, and something skittered through his teeth. He turned back to Ron. "Now can we get this over with, please? I have other souls to eternally torment."

Ephra sank back against the wall, trying to form a coherent thought. "Other souls?" he said. "I'm, I'm dead?"

"No, Ephra. You're very much alive," Ron said. "It's

just that Hades here, for some stupid reason, decided to resurrect you and treat you like a play toy."

Halwyn, or Hades, or whatever his name was, threw up his arms. "What? Gods can't have a little fun anymore?"

"How long have I been writing novels?" Ephra whispered. It was a stupid question, he knew, but it was the only one he could piece together.

Hades laughed. "Since the 1950's, so a fair old while. Before that, though, I had you killed multiple times during the World Wars. They were really quite excellent, while they lasted. Ares did a fantastic job of making them perfect little torture chambers."

"Why would you –"

"Because, *Sisyphus*, when you tie the Lord of the Underworld up with his own chains, he's *bound* to get a little inventive."

Ephra suddenly felt very dizzy. Memories, things he'd thought were only nightmares, began to tumble through his mind. He fell. Ron caught him in time to stop him from slamming into the pavement, but Ephra let out a howl of pain, regardless.

Millennia of torture ripped through him: countless years of being caged and alone, of dying meaningless deaths, any attempt at connection thwarted by Hades' unseen hands. After that came the boulder: centuries upon centuries of lifting its great weight and watching it fall, of blistered fingers, crushed feet, and a broken back. Never was he allowed to stop, not once.

Finally, at the bottom of it all, he found the memories of King Sisyphus of Ephyra.

"We have guests approaching, my love," said Merope.

Sisyphus turned to her, a wicked grin on his face. There was a bubbling feeling in his stomach, one of laughter and excitement, but not at the thought of meeting new friends or hearing the news of travellers. He pressed his thumbs to his forefingers so hard that they made an eerie clicking noise as his skin grated over itself.

Merope looked at him, her face drained. "Please, Sisyphus, once was enough. If you do it again people will know it's you. And we don't even know who these visitors are! You could start a war, anger the gods, ruin Ephyra! That Zeus himself has not already claimed your head –"

Sisyphus cackled. "My dear, not two hours ago in the square, I was mocked for wearing the myrtle wreath you made to show your affection and my status. These people should honour their king as they honour their gods. As they do not seem to know that, I must teach them."

"You want fear, not worship."

He shrugged. "I'm sure Zeus would agree that there is no difference."

"Sisyphus, please."

"I will do as I wish with whoever comes through my doors, and I will let the men and gods of this city know where the power lives in this place." He spoke with a hiss and such an intense glare that Merope seemed to shrink before him. "Now go and tell the kitchen to prepare food and wine."

She nodded and staggered out of the room. Sisyphus took a breath, revelling in his own strength, his own wisdom.

There was a knock at the door and Sisyphus bade his visitors enter. A servant ushered in two strangers. Sisyphus stood and offered his hand in greeting. "Welcome to my home, good friends. Sustenance is on its way. Please, take a seat at my table."

The two men shook his hand. "I'm Aléxandros and this is my brother, Drakon," said the first man. "Thank you for offering us your hospitality."

Sisyphus grinned. "The pleasure is all mine. I hope you will enjoy your time here. It's always a joy to have visitors."

Aléxandros and Drakon took their seats. As Sisyphus wandered back to his at the end of the table, Merope returned with a servant, carrying a jug of wine *and a board of bread, meats and cheeses. The food was placed between the two guests, and the wine decanted into their goblets. Merope brought Sisyphus the rest of the jug so he could help himself.*

He sneered and pushed the jug away. She thinks if she can calm me with wine, I might not go through with the act.

"Will you not drink with us, King Sisyphus?" asked Drakon.

"I'm afraid my innards are not yet ready for more wine. I have indulged my thirst too much today." He smiled. "And besides, a King must be present enough to hear the news of his visitors. Although, not until you've eaten and made any further requests you might have, of course."

"Of course. You're an excellent host! And I can understand your indulgence, Majesty. This wine is most splendid." Aléxandros raised his cup. Sisyphus nodded appreciatively.

They made general conversation while the brothers ate. Aléxandros asked Sisyphus questions about the city and its founding; Drakon asked how he met his beautiful wife and how his sons were. Sisyphus answered all their questions, sometimes truthfully, sometimes with lies so flagrant Merope looked at him in horror from her solitary corner, where she sat stitching. That scared look stirred something in him. He fed off her anticipation of what was to come.

When the visitors were finally full to the brim, Aléxandros smiled and said, "Before we offer our news from afar, we do have one small request."

"And what might that be?"

"We require an escort for the final stretch of our journey," Drakon explained. "There are thieves along the route who could easily overpower just the two of us."

"In return, we will of course welcome you to our dinner table, whenever you might need it," said Aléxandros.

Sisyphus nodded and got to his feet. "I see, I see." He wandered around the table and said, "I believe I have the time to see you to your final destination myself, young sirs."

"Oh, no! We cannot ask a king to do that. One of your servants will suffice."

Sisyphus picked up the knives the men had used to cut the meat and bread. He punctured a leftover piece of cheese with the tip of one and removed it with his teeth. "Honestly, my new friends, it would be my pleasure to help you to your journey's end."

They smiled up at him.

"Then we look forward to travelling with you!" said Drakon.

"Indeed!"

Sisyphus grinned, let out a thunderous laugh, and

stabbed them both in unison.

When the brothers were dead, Sisyphus placed the knives amongst the leftovers and took his seat at the table once more.

Soft sobs sprang from Merope in the corner. Sisyphus breathed deeply.

"My dear, the act is done. And I would and will do it again, until this world learns to respect me for the god I am." Merope wept a little louder. Sisyphus let out a snarl and roared, "Someone get me a guard! These fools need to be on display by sunrise!"

There was a scuffle of feet and a shriek as one of the servants caught sight of the bodies. Sisyphus rubbed his thumb and forefingers together again. This time, they slid over one another without a sound.

Ephra's hands were shaking fiercely as his mind tumbled back to the present. He stared at them, trying to blink away the bloodlust, the royal indignance, the absolute insanity of the man he'd once been.

He sobbed loudly into Ron's lap, completely losing the will to keep himself together.

Ron stroked his hair gently. "I'm sorry, Ephra. I'm so sorry."

"Oh, shut up, Charon!" Hades spat. "That fool doesn't deserve your pity and I'm still trying to wrap my head around how he seems to have won your love."

"He may not have deserved my pity millennia ago, Hades, but I think he stopped being Sisyphus several lives back."

Hades snorted. "Is that your excuse for not recognising him, hey? You used to pride yourself in knowing the face of every spirit to toss you an obol."

Ron didn't stop stroking Ephra's head, but Ephra felt him tense with anger. "I didn't ferry Sisyphus' soul to the Underworld. You did, remember?!"

There was a long silence. Ephra's whole body shivered, but he lifted himself from Ron's lap and looked him in the eye.

"You're the ferryman?"

Ron nodded. "I really just look after Styx now, oversee and record oaths made in front of her."

Ephra swallowed, pulling the knowledge from Sisyphus' memories. "Because breaking an oath made over the Styx has consequences." He turned to Hades, stitching his thoughts together with some agony. "So you can't make me break the oath I made, and you can't make Ron do it either."

Hades set his lips in a hard line. "No, I can't make you break it, but I can throw you into the Styx and let the souls of the damned tear you to pieces if one of you

143

doesn't."

Ephra took a deep breath. His whole body hurt. He already felt like he'd been taken apart and then rammed back together again. He got to his feet and offered Ron a hand. Ron took it. As Ephra pulled him up. He caught Ron's face in his free palm and said, "You know everything I did, who I was?"

"Yes," Ron said. "I heard the stories. Sisyphus was quite the celebrity amongst us lesser gods."

Ephra shuddered, pushing down the image of blood on his hands, the taste in his mouth. He swallowed again. "And knowing all that, do you still love me?"

Ron opened his mouth. He hesitated, glancing at Hades. Ephra squeezed his hand. Ron tore his eyes away from the death god and said, "Of course I love you, Ephra, but Hades is –"

"I love you, too," Ephra interjected and kissed Ron quickly and with as much love as he could muster, because he very much suspected it might be their last.

"Time, people! I have other places to be!" Hades yelled.

Ephra spun on his heel. "I'm not breaking my oath, and neither is Ron. So you can throw me into the Styx and we'll see what happens."

Hades let out an almighty growl, sparks flying from his hair. He launched himself at Ephra, picking him up with the greatest of ease, and flung him into the river.

The wind whistled sharply against Ephra's eardrums and then his body buckled into the ice cold water of the Styx. He tried to pull himself to the surface, kicking and flailing awkwardly, but ghostly hands reached up and began to tug him down and down, further into the murky water. As he struggled, faces lurched at him madly; lost souls twisted him this way and that with rage.

Please, Sticks, Ephra thought, *I don't want to leave Ron. I don't want to break my promise. Please, Sticks. Styx!*

Something strong and muscular twisted itself around Ephra's ankle. At first he thought it was a water plant, that he'd reached the bottom where he would remain until he could no longer hold his breath. His lungs were already burning with effort, trying to milk every last drop of oxygen out of his final desperate gasp of air. Then Ephra realised that he was being dragged in parallel to the light of the surface. No, not entirely parallel. He was getting closer to the light, too.

Ethereal fingers scraped at his skin, trying to get a grip, but whatever was towing him was far stronger. Then, all at once, he was thrown up onto the bank and his ears were filled with a vicious hissing. Ephra looked up. In front of him sat Sticks. Only she wasn't the four-foot critter that had watched him from her tank. Ephra couldn't really take in how big she was exactly. Her enormous body was still partially draped into the water, where souls cowered back into the waves at the sound of her voice. Her head, though, that Ephra could see, and it was at least three times the size of Ephra's own dainty skull.

Eventually, she closed her great mouth and looked at him. She brought her nose to his face, staring at him expectantly. Ephra reached out a tentative hand and she pressed her snout against it. He shivered with relief. Her giant tongue slapped at his palm.

"Thank you, Sticks," Ephra said, "Thank you, thank you."

Ephra pulled himself fully up onto the bank and lay down for a moment, trying to catch his breath. Sticks placed her great beady eye next to his face. He watched silver waters shimmer within it.

"So, you're a goddess and a river, huh?" Ephra breathed. "What's that like?"

She smiled, a genuine smile, and let out what sounded like a laugh. Ephra placed his hand on her head and scratched her brow.

"I should get back up there, but I don't know if my legs will carry me." Ephra whispered.

Sticks shoved her snout into his side.

"Yeah, okay. They will." Ephra laughed.

He stood up gingerly. Sticks let him use her head to steady himself. When he was balanced, he looked at her and asked, "Did you know who I was this whole time?"

Sticks nodded.

"Sisyphus never met Ron – *Charon* – before, but you did." Ephra looked down into the soul-filled waters. "Hades dragged him through you when he took him down the first time." He remembered Sisyphus gasping for air, lungs flooding with water, skin burning from Hades' fire. Breaking down and telling himself he deserved it all.

Ephra almost fell once more, but Sticks pushed her muscular body flat against his side.

"Sorry," Ephra said. "Sorry, I feel as if I don't quite know who I am right now."

Sticks rubbed her cheek against his face, then she let out a hiss that sounded vaguely like, "Ephra."

"Ephra?" he asked. "You really think I'm just Ephra Stone?"

She smiled. "No jussst about it."

Ephra swallowed. It was still a lot to process: his soul was ancient, it had done awful things and had had awful things done to it, the man he loved was a god, the man he hated was the ruler of the Underworld. Still, something about having a vote of confidence from a gigantic snake goddess did steady Ephra's nerves.

"Okay then," he said. "Time to face the music."

Sticks slapped his face with her tongue and Ephra smiled a little. As he began to plod back up towards the bridge, with Sticks nudging him along, a bird landed on his shoulder. He recognised its speckled chest and fluffy feathers.

"Nice to see you again, Mr Song Thrush," he said with a sigh. "It's been a while."

The bird chirped and it sounded an awful lot like, "Nice to see you, too."

Ephra stopped in his tracks, Sticks almost knocking him off his feet. "Hang on!" he said, then to the thrush, "You can understand me?"

"Yes, of course," the song thrush sang, tilting its head in confusion. "Did you really not know? The parakeets said this incarnation seemed a bit thick, but I just thought you were pretending."

Ephra stared at the bird, his mind unravelling a little bit further. Then Sticks gave him a good shove. "Sorry, sorry. No, this shouldn't really be such a surprise. It's just ... today's *a lot*."

The thrush nodded with understanding. "So I gather. Was that Hades I saw throwing you into the river?"

"Yes." Ephra replied. "Why?"

The bird chutted thoughtfully for a moment, then chirped something that sounded like, "I'll be back," and fluttered away.

Ephra stood, trying to process what the song thrush had been twittering to itself. It was like trying to translate the mutterings of a native speaker when he'd only just learnt the basics of the language. But he got there, and he laughed with relief.

Everything is going to be okay.

As they came into view, Ephra could see the sparks flying off the top of Hades' head. He was paler than before, his eyes like festering coal. Ron, however, was suppressing a smile. The corners of his lips betrayed him when they got close enough. He winked at Ephra.

"Styx," Hades began quietly. "Since when did you interfere in my business?"

Hades raised his eyes and Ephra knew that Sticks was now towering above them all. She remained silent, so Ephra spoke for her, "Since you started interfering in hers. I made her an oath and I didn't want to break it, so she helped."

Hades glared at him in response. "And what? Now you've taken a dunk and got full-body invulnerability, you think I'm not going to be able to torture you? Sisyphus, my dear boyo, I've got more vile tricks up my sleeve yet."

Ephra peered up at Sticks. "Invulnerable?"

Sticks smiled and nodded.

Ephra took a breath, then squared his shoulders and turned back to Hades. "Hades, I don't know how to break this to you, but Ron's right. I'm not Sisyphus anymore," he said firmly. "You tortured and killed him so many times that he fractured and became something new."

"We'll see about that when I'm done pouring lava down your gullet." Hades grinned.

Ephra shook his head. "No, I'm not going back to the Underworld with you. And before you say it, I'm not writing you any more novels. Thousands of years' worth of punishment is quite enough. So I swear –"

"*You swear*?" Hades belted. "You swear! You swear?!" He tore across the pavement towards Ephra, fire blazing from his scalp, but Sticks let out a furious hiss. Hades stopped sharply, a few feet from Ephra, and took a giant step back. "What do you swear?" he growled.

"I swear, Hades, if you come near me, or Ron, or Sticks again, I will smite you down."

Hades tipped back his head and let out an almighty cackle. It took him a moment to recover, but Ephra didn't flinch. He held onto his breath and stared the god down. Hades narrowed his eyes. "And you say you're not Sisyphus, the man who would be a god? Smite me, will you, Ephra Stone? With what god-given gifts are you expecting to do that, exactly?"

At that precise moment, the song thrush landed on Ephra's shoulder and chirped into his ear. He petted it gently, then pointed at the sky. "The one you gave me, Hades." They all looked up at the sky together. Swirling like an angry tornado above their heads was a mass of birds. There were thousands of them, twisting and turning in perfect formation. "It turns out I've been helping out birds for many of my lives, and they've grown to rather enjoy my company. Think we really started to understand each other somewhere around World War One, when I saved a heron at the Somme."

"You can speak to them?" Hades looked surprised for a second, then he snorted. "Still, you really think a bunch of birds are going to scare me? I'm a death god, Ephra."

Ephra looked at Ron. Ron nodded and took a step toward him. The crack of lightning was so close and so bright that Ephra had to close his eyes. When he opened them again, the figure that stood next to him was twice Ron's previous size and wielding an oar made entirely of skulls.

"I also made a promise I wouldn't let Ephra go, Hades, so you'll have to get through me and the birds."

"Charon..." Hades growled.

"And what about you, Styx? Would you help Ephra

keep his oath, too?"

Ephra looked at Sticks. She appeared to have grown even more since he last glanced at her. She tilted her head cockily and said, "I sssswear."

Ephra laughed and stroked her scaly body. Then he turned back to Hades. "Are we done?"

The birds above swirled down and around Hades, landing on every surface available.

Hades let out an almighty roar and a column of flame enveloped him. "You're invulnerable, Ephra Stone, not immortal, and when you die again, I will personally see you burn for this."

"I don't know about that, Hades," Ephra replied. "I rather think that when I die, your psychopomp here will take me somewhere sunny to live out the rest of our eternity together."

There was another roar and then Hades disappeared with a blast that knocked Ephra off his feet.

When he came to, a normal-sized Ron and a normal-sized Sticks were peering down at him.

"Are you okay?" Ron asked.

Ephra beamed dizzily. "I'm better than okay," he said. "I'm free." He pressed his hand to Ron's face. "And I love you."

Sticks butted him with her nose.

"And you, too, Sticks. I love you, too."

Officially speaking, Ephra moved in with Ron about six months after they first met, but Ephra didn't really have to move much out of his flat in Bayswater by the time his contract ended. It was really more a matter of handing the keys over.

After that, they lived in a nervous sort of bliss. Most of the gods that visited Ron's apartment for 'mediation' greeted Ephra quite politely. Some even shook his hand, cracked jokes with him, and said it was about time someone took Hades down a peg or two.

Still, Ephra couldn't help but feel uneasy. Mrs Z – or Hera, as he quickly realised after retrieving Sisyphus' memory – did not return. Ron said not to worry, but everyone knew that Hera had always been the type to hold a grudge. Hell, half of Greek 'mythology' was Zeus being an ass and Hera raining wrath down on everyone involved. If she hadn't returned for further supernatural mediation, then either she had let all her grudges go, or she and Zeus were still angry about what Ephra's soul had done millennia ago.

It took Ephra a good two years to finally begin to relax. In those two years, he stayed productive, though. He managed to write and sell three novels, and every single one was a romance. Despite his remarks about hating the genre, when Ephra went to put pen to paper again, he found romance was all he wanted to write. And this time, every book came from the heart.

Readers seemed to notice it, too. His first book published out from under Hades' thumb gained quite a bit of traction. On the back of its success, his next manuscript sold for the kind of advance Ephra had never even dreamed of making. As for the third, well, it had sat on the bestseller list for six weeks, which wasn't too shabby.

Ephra sat in a bookshop, taking a quick sip from a bottle of water, mulling over his success. He was staring at a queue of people waiting for him to sign book number four.

If you'd told me this was where I'd be two years ago, I'd have laughed in your face, he thought. *Everything seems so much more vivid now.*

He put down his water and waved to the next person in the queue. The young woman came bounding up to the desk, asked him how he came up with his ideas, and told him to make the inscription out to Katie. Ephra obliged, and was in the middle of saying something about drawing inspiration from real life when a bolt of lightning hit the street outside the shop.

Ephra jumped as the thunder rumbled. He squeezed the pen in his grip and counted to ten, then smiled at the girl. It was a cloudy, rainy day. Lightning was perfectly normal.

"Sorry," he said. "I'm a bit of scaredy-cat when it comes to lightning."

The girl seemed to swoon a little, then she thanked him very much and dashed towards a group of friends standing in the non-fiction section.

Ephra's mouth had gone dry in his moment of panic, so he fumbled with his water bottle to take another quick swig. As he did so, a large man with a great white beard stepped up to the table and placed down a copy of his book.

"I like this one a great deal," he said. "It's one of your best."

"Thank you." Ephra smiled weakly. "I like to think I get better with age."

"Oh, you definitely have!"

Ephra put his water down, picked up a pen and flicked to the title page. "Who shall I make this out to?"

"Zeus."

Ephra dropped the pen immediately, eyes snapping up. He took the man's face in again. It had been a long time since he'd seen the King of the Gods, and he hadn't recognised him in his modern grey suit. Ephra dipped his head. "It's g-good to see you, sir," he stuttered.

"Ephra!" Zeus laughed. "Please, relax. I only came for an autograph." Ephra peered up at him. "I promise."

Ephra picked up his pen with a shaky hand and began writing out the inscription carefully.

"You made quite a fool of my brother ... again," Zeus said in a jovial tone. "I really thought he'd blast you to oblivion, but you did a wonderful job of making that basically impossible."

"I didn't mean to make a fool of him. It was just, I ... I made an oath to Styx and –"

"Oh, don't worry about it!" Zeus patted Ephra's shoulder and Ephra felt his skin tingle with electricity. "If I'd been bothered about it I would have come to see you much sooner."

Ephra let out a shuddery breath. "So why are you here?"

Zeus perched on the edge of the table and it creaked under his great weight. "I wanted to see you, or I guess meet you, really. And I wanted to make sure that you actually get it this time."

Ephra tried to straighten up, to look Zeus in the eye. "Get what, sir?"

"That there should be no more out-smarting, no more cunning, no more chaining up gods in the Underworld."

"Absolutely not," Ephra said firmly. "I think you know, sir, but Sisyphus is dead and buried under many, many boulders. I'm Ephra Stone and all I want in this world is a man named Ron."

Zeus studied him, looking into the depths of his soul with such a gaze that Ephra could almost feel its probing. Then the god chortled to himself and clapped his hands. "Well then, the king is dead, long live the man!" He rocked up onto his feet and the table swayed with him. "Are you finished signing?"

"Yes, sir." Ephra handed Zeus his book.

"This one is set up for a sequel, yes?"

Ephra nodded.

"I look forward to it. You know, Hera and I read these new ones together. They really are inspired." Zeus smiled kindly. "You can see how much you love him. You look like an entirely different man."

"Thank you, sir."

"I hear your prayers, too, you know." Zeus' gaze grew suddenly steely and Ephra thought he might just keel over. "You do have my blessing." Zeus winked.

Ephra felt his whole chest expand, a torrent of joy bubbling up from his gut to his throat. "*Thank you, sir,*" he squeaked.

Zeus let out a thunderous laugh, and with a flash of lightning, was gone.

As the sound of general chatter returned to the room, Ephra sat back in his seat. He slipped his hand into the pocket of his coat and ran his thumb over the small velvet box inside. He had a romantic boat trip to plan.

Acknowledgements

My first *Labours of Stone* thank you goes to Tori, Queen of Commas and Heir to Hyphens (we've decided she gets a new title every time she edits for me), for telling my incredibly anxious, freshly-traumatized self that my first draft was actually wonderful to read and definitely worth working on.

Thanks also to the rest of the Clubamabob lot for all your insight and support in developing this little book. I hope you know I'm eagerly awaiting the day I get to pass on the publication crown! I can't wait to hold your bookchildren in my grubby mitts.

Thank you to Amy for helping me find the best coffee in the weirdest place, and for all our lovely walks around the parks of London. I hope, someday (after the Great Panna Cotta has finally been thrown out), we get to wander up the Serpentine together again.

To all the lovely humans of the online writing community, including my wonderful UK writing peeps and my best ghost ffrind, thank you so much for everything you do – for all the advice, support and love – it really means so, so much!

To my family, who find themselves living with the crazed entity I call "me" once more, thank you for bearing with me through the ups and downs of the last eighteen months. And specifically to Dad: thanks for not dying.

Kit, you're the bestest boy and I love you. Thank you for reminding me to eat lunch, every day at 12PM on the dot.

And finally ... to this book ... to Ephra, Ron, Sticks and even Halwyn: thank you for being the story that I got to write when I was at my worst. Thank you for giving me a space to think and laugh. And thank you for keeping me company at 2AM.

About the Author

EM Harding is a queer author who hails from Wales. They started writing seriously at the age of eight (they were a very serious child) and received their first rejection letter around the age of nine. EM now holds a BA in English with Creative Writing and an MA in Applied Linguistics (both from the University of Birmingham). They run a writing group known as "The Writeryjig Clubamabob" – a name that even EM can't spell without looking it up – and they're an active member of the Twitter #WritingCommunity.

They are also guardian to an illustrious chicken thief named Kit.

Labours of Stone is EM's second novella. Much the same as the first one, it was a wild ride (particularly with the whole worldwide panini situation going on) and EM will now be napping for the foreseeable future.

By the Same Author

Moon-Sitting

The Moon fell into the Ocean and the Waves wept.

Infinity was once home to a thriving civilisation. That is, before the Moon arrived. The enormous, spherical structure brought with it death and destruction, wiping out most of the population with a series of earthquakes and tsunamis.

Since then the Moon has sat silently on the southern edge of Infinity's mass continent.

Lucky Marsh is one of three moon-sitters charged with monitoring the Moon, acting as a living alarm system for Infinity's last city. They must watch, but never touch: that's the golden rule of moon-sitting. However, for the ever-curious Lucky, that rule has become increasingly difficult to abide.

Her nightmares compel her to do more. Her feet betray her while she sleeps.

Printed in Great Britain
by Amazon